PUB FICTION

Edited By Leonie Stevens

ALLEN & UNWIN

Publication of this title was assisted by The Australia Council,
the Federal Government's arts funding and advisory body.

O⌐
Australia **Council**
for the Arts

First published in 1997 by
Allen & Unwin
9 Atchison Street
St Leonards NSW 2065
Australia
Phone: (61 2) 9901 4088
Fax: (61 2) 9906 2218
E-mail: frontdesk@allen-unwin.com.au
URL: http://www.allen-unwin.com.au

National Library of Australia
Cataloguing-in-Publication:

Pub fiction.

  ISBN 1 86448 211 7.

  1. Bars (Drinking establishments)—Fiction. 2. Short
  stories, Australian—20th century. I. Stevens, Leonie,
  1962– . II. Title.

A823.0108355

Set in 11/13 pt Times by DOCUPRO, Sydney
Printed and bound by Australian Print Group,
Maryborough, Victoria.

10 9 8 7 6 5 4 3 2 1

CONTENTS

PUB FICTION

INTRODUCTION

The concept arose, not out of the blue, but out of the smoke. One of those lazy afternoons, those lazy sessions (you know the kind)—hey, someone should do an anthology called *Pub Fiction*. Yeah—get a bunch of cool writers. They'll know what to do. Make it fun—ask them to contribute a graphic. Get funky packaging. Don't spoon-feed connections and possibilities. Don't over-edit. Keep it raw. Keep it authentic. Don't bow to any tired old literary ideals. Forget the critics: entertain the readers.

The result you hold in your hand.

Pub Fiction—stories short and tall, icy and neat.

PUB FICTION

Now if you don't dig wordy introductions, head straight for the bar. For slower immersion, find yourself a table, make sure it's not wet and read on . . .

You're trying to hold on to your dream, but everyone tells you, nah, this ain't gonna work. One day you'll prove them wrong. You'll make them look the fools. One day—

Writers today are a multi-skilled lot. Many of the contributors to *Pub Fiction* are also busy with music, film, art, performance. That's why the title, an obvious pun on Quentin Tarantino's *Pulp Fiction*, made so much immediate sense. We are children of television: we are informed by pop culture. Music and film are an integral part of the creative process.

You spend all day racing round inner Sydney, searching for the one that you want. They say try the Rose, nah, try Kevin's. When you finally find him, what do you do?

You go to the pub, of course.

In his introduction to the screenplay of *True Romance*, Tarantino said 'I guess what I'm always trying to do is use these [answers first/questions later] structures that I see in novels and apply them to cinema.' Likewise, many writers today are also working on ways to bring cinematic qualities to literature. We write in scenes: our chapters are episodes.

It's hell on a weeknight, just the same old bunch of drunken fools and losers, till a simple gesture stuns you, proving that romance does exist.

INTRODUCTION

Pub Fiction brings the pubs and clubs of Australia (and elsewhere) to life.
Hear the beer-soaked carpet.
Smell conversations from the next table.
Taste the menace.

Your girlfriend's off with her ex, and you're trying to stay cool, but you're haunted by the guy you know who went on a murderous jealous rampage . . . could you do it too?

These stories play out over a landscape of ideas, locations and states of mind. For the purposes of this collection, PUB translates beyond the traditional Local to clubs, casinos, strip joints, bottle shops. The cultural centres: the legalised drug hangouts. These are snapshots, moments, *feelings*—

You're supposed to chant, 'I want none of this involvement', but even at the pub, the greyhounds look like work.

Or else

You've got no choice. It's your living. You're trying to get through a five-night gig. You've got to perform, be sensational, but you can't even go to the chemist without getting kidnapped in an armed robbery. . .

Not always the place of relaxation. Not always the sanctuary.

You get angry because HE promised to cook if YOU went to the bottle shop. You sense the outrage, but you keep yelling and you don't stop until—

PUB FICTION

Anything goes. The pub, the temple, the site of resistance

It's the one day of the year when no-one's gonna dare hassle you for having green hair. It's power day, solidarity day. Now, as for the other 364. . .

and host to redemption.

He's back. The problems that drove you apart don't seem so crucial. An old country pub, just the two of you . . . it could work out this time. It really could.

Familiar?

The performance bummed out, so you go with your mates to the crappiest club in town. The ethical one in your crowd is aghast, but exactly where is the sleaze?

The generic and the quirky. The second home and the cesspit.

Home is the other side of the world. Everyone's alien. In the dark after closing, he says, 'Don't breathe a word'. He says it as a threat.

All those hours spent sitting, dreaming. The types. The moments of illumination. The muddy ruminations. The gallantry and pathos. Life in a nutshell. The absolute pits. Pub as the site of delightful surprise,

One day you're going to get out of there. One day, they'll come to take you home. You need a release, an escape, a rescue—

INTRODUCTION

gut-wrenching cliché

*You're the vomit-specked urine-dampened fool they all
expect you to be. And you don't care.*

and downright fear.

*He says you're part of the conspiracy, and you laugh,
but the demons won't be shaken loose. Madness fills the
air . . .*

Thirsty?

One final word. Don't go calling *us* grunge. Not lit-grit,
or on the edge, or any of those perverted generalisations.
Dirty realism? Oh, dear.
Look to thyself, gentle reader.
We are *all* bacteria.
If there's grit in these stories,
that's the nature of the site.
And life.
These are *real* stories, that's all.
Little episodes from the big picture.
Enjoy.

Leonie Stevens, 1996

LEGEND: t – Won at track. d – Won this trip on another course.
b – Beaten favourite last start.
c – Won here over this distance. ★ – Spell of 3 months. h – Home track.
m – Won on wet track. ★ – Spell of 3 months. h – Home track.

TRICOM AUDIOTEXT (Rate: 25¢ buys 21.4 secs.)

1-12.20 Healthy Diet-Try It Hcp 1200m

Race 1: Results/Dividends Tel: 0055 33751.

(Two-Year-Olds. Apprentices can claim)
Of $6,000; 1st $3,900; 2nd $1,200; 3rd $600; 4th $300.

No	Form	Horse	Jockey	Weight
1-	1 3 5 4	BISCA-GO-GO b (8)	(a) E Cassar	57.5
2-	7 ★ 3	FUSTIAN (11)	G Skinner	55
3-		APPARATUS (12)	J O Walsh	54
4-		L'AVENIR (14)	D Brereton	54
5-		OUR RACING DREAM (9)	D Duric	54
6-		THONG UTHAI h (3)	P Mertens	54
6-		MY SPECIAL BOY h (13)	A Findlay	53
7-	0	AGELESS BEAUTY (1)	(a) A Prebble	52.5
8-	9 2	CATRIONA (6)	J Matthews	52.5
8-	3	MUSIC BOUTIQUE	(a) Travis Harrison	52.5
10-	9	STAR OF VALIMA (2)	(a) Craig Williams	52
11-	7	PRINCESS NATALIE (4)	S Baster	52
12-	9	GOT PERMISSION (10)	S Noll	52
14-	8	STARS APPEAR h (7)	C Dinn	52

APPARATUS 1 Bisca-Go-Go 2 Music Boutique 3

BETTING: 4 Apparatus 5 Music Boutique 6
Bisca-Go-Go, Catriona 7 Fustian 10 Our Racing Dream,
Ageless Beauty, Star Of Valima 12 Thong Uthai 14
Ageless Beauty, Star Of Valima 33 My Special Boy 50 Got

---

the‸.
S'dow‸.
Poetique ‸.
form and tak‸.

MOBILE LINK
galloper with great s‸.
Spirit Of Remlap 1300m‸.
1½len win Top Lunch, Dane‸.
21. A Group III winner in Per‸.

BIONIC BESS (A Noonan) 4m 2‸.
2len win Cyclone Watch 1600m S'do‸.
25 and then eased near 400m for 4le‸.
1800m Ascot Fruit'n'veg Stk Dec 2. Ret‸.
failed stint in Perth. Should be thereabouts.

TAMBUN LAD (P J Clarke) 4g 13; 4-0-5: Res‸.
with ¼len 3rd 1000m MV Dec 9 then inquiry in‸.
performance after 4½len, 8th (7.4f) Ben's Rocket‸.
1200m S'down Christmas Hcp Dec 26 before 2len 3rd
Skipper Regent 1200m S'down Jan 27. Give thou‸.

DELSOLE (G Marconi) 4g 48; 3-11-4: In th‸.
when 3len 7th Hunza Court 1433m Flem Ma‸.
Feb then broke through for overdue victory ‸.
Stately Bay, Ngawapurua 1200m MV ‸.
11. Tries hard but rarely wins.

NAVY BRASS (G A Ryan) 4g ‸.
when 3¾len 9th Virtual Reali‸.
6 before ¼len 3rd Prince ‸.
Wit Feb 3. In top ‸.

PARIHAKA ‸.
galloper. C‸.
Protar‸.

LIKE LOVERS IMMORTAL

Helen Barnes

I've been working in this bar too long and I've started to see things. If you worked here, you'd start to see things too. Anything to escape what is actually before your eyes. Tuesday night at 'The Track' bar of the Eureka Hotel is the closest you can get to Hell on a weeknight. Don't get too excited. It's one of the banal levels of Hell, for people who haven't been all that bad, but haven't been particularly good either.

It's a grey plaster render stage of Hades. In every corner, there is Sky Channel on the television. On a veneer scroll above the bar, the name of every Melbourne Cup winner since 1901 is inscribed in gold leaf. In the men's toilet, above the piss trough, is inscribed the name of every loser who's drunk here since 1978. I don't know what medium is used.

The time moves so slow that sometimes it doesn't move at all. Sometimes it moves backwards. From the high window I see the moon suspended in a matt black sky. This is as close to the elements as I get.

My shift started at one. I've seen the sun through the high window at its peak and through its descent into the bruised purple and yellow of sunset. Steph, the other barmaid, and I have both been on since one. We stand side by side on either side of the till, arms crossed, taking it in turns to sigh.

There are about twenty punters littered around the bar, smoking like ash heaps. They have nothing to say except for their murmured prayers to the gambling gods who never seem to look their way, as they finger the slips in their tracksuit pants. In between races, they gnaw on congealed chops and peas that have sat in the bain marie for two hours or more, and when they need a piss they take their beer with them, because they don't trust anyone these days.

It's the sport of kings, this racing business.

The bar stewards clocked on at two to clean up after the lunch rush. They're all South American. That's a mystery. The first one to arrive was André, a huge, flat-faced man with hands the size of dinner plates. It seems that he sponsored the rest—Harry with the drooping black and grey moustache, Yosef with the high rosy cheekbones, and Nestor who speaks no English and is always singing Latin pop songs. He's like a postcard. They're from Chile and Nicaragua, all over the shop. Yosef is from El Salvador, he's a doctor. He told me one night that he preferred cleaning ashtrays and mopping up honest drunk vomit to picking bullets out of children and old people. There's not a lot a girl from the suburbs can say to a remark like that. Things are not tough all over. Not at all.

A middle-aged couple have been in the bar since the third weight-for-age at Flemington. They're set up at a table in the corner with all the little luxuries of their lives. This week's 'Wizard', betting slips, the yellow form guide out of Saturday's *Age*, a middy and a schooner of draught on the half hour, and a packet of those cigarettes that they only sell in lots of fifty. The ones with clouds and birds and shit like that on the pack.

If they've seen better days there's no sign of it. He's an old delinquent, with tattoos on his knuckles. Faded now, they look like superfluous veins.

Boy is his name, or that's what she calls him. He's an over-ripe yob, no callow youth, with his hair as black as boot polish, greased back with Elvis Presley pretensions. The scab of a split lip catches on his fag whenever he takes a drag. Raelene wears a screaming purple leisure suit with bright white Korean cross-trainers. She's just had her highlights done, and it looks like the ends of her pot scourer hair have been torched with a soldering iron.

The stewards bring their own tapes to work and between the races and the country and western songs on the jukebox is *Ruben Blades: Metienda Maño*.

Raelene and her Boy take it in turns to scuttle around to the TAB next door and they discuss each race as if they owned the bloodstock. 'Shoulda trained 'im in the wet,' Boy says, frowning with concern, 'They never train 'em in the wet before they bring 'em down to Melbourne.' Raelene clucks, sighs and shrugs, looking up at him with clear, green eyes. She hangs off his words as if it was honey that dripped from his lips, not fag ash.

André comes up and says, 'Hey, did you know Nestor was a Sandinista?'

5

'Nestor, singing to his broom over there? Oh, right.'

'It's true,' and for a moment we stare at Nestor, sweeping up the ash behind the potted palms. Can we see him crawling on his belly on the floral carpet of the hotel? Just about. Been working here far too long.

At three, Rae and Boy have a feed of steak and chips, and she laughs at his jokes. 'Darl, you oughta be on the bloody telly!' she shrieks.

After the last race, Boy curses Darren Gauci, 'Every time I put me money on that bastard he chokes. Every single bloody time. He's a fucking prick.' Raelene smears another layer of apricot cream lipstick on her mouth. It's her round. She smiles at me while I pour the beer, and I see the sticky mess is on her porcelain front teeth as well. As I count the change, she is at least 10 degrees off vertical.

They're the closest to Romeo and Juliet I'm going to get tonight. They are Romeo and Juliet, if those two brainless youths had survived long enough to be disinherited by their families. You've gotta die at fourteen, I want to tell them, sixteen tops. She looks up at him, her pupils little black dots in lime jelly eyes this late in the day. Blind love, it's an eyesore.

But here they are at, I don't know, forty-something, with livers the size of footballs, distended beer bellies and nicotine-stained fingers.

It's now around seven. I've been watching them all this time. I've got nothing else to do except stare at the clock above the saloon doors and watch the time drip away. Every second gone, a second that I'll never have again. Every heartbeat wasted. You're born with a set number programmed into you. A fixed number. So many and then stop. It's enough to make you spit.

The seven o'clock skinny with the stubble head

creeps in, looking around the room with yellow headlight eyes. He's had a number one all over his scabby scalp. His jeans are shrunk. Man, those jeans are severe. His balls must be the size of walnuts. He wears a shrunken old school jumper, showing his shrivelled up belly button.

He puts his change in the jukebox and he puts on 'Space Oddity' every time, then he plays air guitar for a minute or two, acoustic air guitar, how sad is that? 'Psycho killer,' Steph mutters over the top of the sill, 'no doubt about it.' We're just waiting for something to show up in the papers so we can dob him in. The next time anyone gets killed, anywhere, we're dialling 000. We'll say, 'It's the seven o'clock skinny. Throw away the key.'

And the mood changes with Raelene and Boy. The beer bubbles back up and Boy turns mean. She still smiles at him, though her eyes are fixed on some point on the ceiling that she likes the look of. It's her turn on the jukebox, and she picks A64, Charlie Rich. 'That bastard can sing, can't he?' she calls but Boy dismisses her with a wave of his hand, puts his wallet in his pocket and goes to the dunny.

'There's this American heavy metal death ship pulling into Port Phillip Bay tonight with two hundred and something tonnes of radioactive goodwill', Steph tells me. 'I'm against nuclear weapons', she explains. I can understand that. Bombs are pretty superfluous when her boyfriend, Bolt the bouncer, is around. He's a square-shaped, purely functional sort of guy, no trimmings, no ornamentation. Having a verb for a name suits him. It didn't have to be Bolt. Rip would have been just as good. So would Crunch, or Gouge. He assaults our bar every night around eight to pick up Steph. He says, 'Don't keep me waiting, bitch', and kisses her right between the eyes. She says it's true love. I think it's an illusion.

'I didn't know we'd become political, Steph,' I say.

'You have no idea. Those Yanks better not come in here,' Steph declares. 'Wouldn't give 'em a glass of hot piss if they were dying of thirst in the desert.'

Precisely as she says that, the saloon doors burst open and hit the wall behind. Bang. Most of the punters open the door just enough to get their withered carcasses through. Not the sailors. Their faces are already red, and their form is solid and black and unassailable even in their ridiculous trousers.

They are huge and happy, red-faced and congenial. They look like aliens. With voices that make all the glasses shake, they shout hello and slap backs indiscriminately, yelling, 'Hey, look at all these little Ossies. Can you guys sing "Waltzing Matilda" for us?'

A cringing silence follows. The punters push their plates of chips and sauce away, wipe their wet lips. They aren't political. They aren't activists. They're just ashamed of themselves, so shabby and feeble.

Raelene's legs are getting away from her as she hammers on the jukebox. The Yanks have started to sing 'King of the Road'. Her hips suddenly give to the left while her feet remain just where she put them. Bringing her hips back in plumb line, she then sways to the right, like she's doing some kind of slow motion tango with the record player.

When Boy comes back, he says, 'There's something we need to discuss, Raelene.' She is too far gone to speak, but deflates and bows her back.

'You've been lying to me for years, Raelene,' his voice is thick and oily with poison. 'Lying doesn't become you, Rae.' He settles back on his stool, his mouth set in a crooked line. Like a smack in the head, it seems to come from nowhere.

'Oh, Boy,' Raelene says and a deep phlegm-filled cough rattles soggily up her throat. She swallows stoically, gazes at him with wet eyes and the sailors sing. They just won't stop.

Man, that's gotta be love. What else could it be? There's something glinting in the moonlight, even if it sure stinks and you wouldn't want to step in it.

And Ruben keeps singing 'Pablo Pueblo', with all those cow bells, the sharp trombone, the switching beat, as the South American stewards mutter amongst themselves and turn the music up.

It's not the sort of shit you hear on Tragic FM. It's not 'Guentenamera'. It's not Gloria Estefan or anything like that. It's this weird kind of wailing and the clattering of metal and everything and everyone sounds almost but not quite out of tune. Nestor is beside himself with joy as he empties the bin and takes the bottles out one by one to smash them in the dumpster in time to 'La Maleta'. Someone blows a tin whistle all the way through.

'I know what you did with Steve,' Boy continues, 'and I know what you did with Dave,' and she still can't speak but gazes up at the bluish bristle on his chin. He's the whole world to her right now and he's a cruel bastard. 'And I know what you got up to that weekend you couldn't come to Mum's. Don't try to deny it.'

Deny it? I don't think that she can even understand it. But Boy thinks he's got her on the ropes now. Lighting another one of those sawdust cigarettes, he squints into the distance like he thinks he's Clint Eastwood, his eyes mean slits in his brown old handbag face.

Steph pulls me into the store room for a moment. 'I've got a new tattoo. Take a look.' She pinches her jeans down and shows me Caspar the Ghost in angry red–black lines.

'What does it mean?'

'I don't know,' she answers, 'I was gonna get the Pegasus but it was ten dollars more'. I find it hard to believe but here I am looking at it.

My Romeo and Juliet are still there, though he's lowered his voice. He continues his speech, poking the air with his cigarette for punctuation, dribbling ash all over the now useless form guides. And she just sits there, mouth open a bit, lime jelly eyes still gazing up at him.

Outside the grey rendered walls, the moon sits bloated in the sky, looking down without interest, as it always has done, on all our greatest lovers. They went to Hell, most of them. Romeo and Juliet, Antony and Cleopatra, Héloïse and Abelard. Suicides, adulterers, fornicators, punters.

That bloody mariachi music clatters out onto the street and more sailors in black uniforms with laughable trousers reel in. 'Yosef,' I say, 'you must turn this music off. Can't you see it's drawing them?' But Yosef in reply only grabs me round the waist and whirls me round the ice machine and pirouettes out again. 'I think we will be requiring some more tequila,' he says as he goes.

The sailors drink tequila, lemon and salt. Steph and I are charging them double the bar price and pocketing the difference. 'Is this a statement, Steph?' I ask.

She says, 'Yes, it is, we're gonna be rich.'

'It's the lambada, Boy,' Raelene says. It's the first thing she's said for hours and it's wrong. 'You're some dancer, Boy, you know that?' And he nods gravely, yes, he is. Then he clears his throat, drains the last inch of beer from his glass that must be warm by now and ninety per cent spit anyway.

LIKE LOVERS IMMORTAL

Then, and it illuminates my fluoro-lit world like a wanton miracle from the impenetrable night. Boy picks up Raelene's plump and nerveless hands, and, leaving the Wizard and the useless slips and fully half a packet of fags, he wheels her up and off her stool, and they swirl and circle like lovers immortal. Past the Sandinista emptying the ice sink, past the drunken sailors singing 'Barbara Ann', over Ruben Blades singing 'Plantacion Adentro', past me, past Steph and her new tattoo. They float out the saloon doors and into the street invisible, leaving the unmistakable scent of violets in the air, and the fat, bloated moon grins down from the matt black sky.

Maybe he'll slap her around a bit before bedtime. Maybe they'll get Chinese take-away and fall asleep in front of the television. Maybe they'll take off their clothes and dance naked in the moonlight.

Maybe they'll escape to a less tedious region of the underworld.

Maybe I'm seeing things.

Or true love is a smack between the eyes and leaving half a packet of fags behind you. They were old and ugly with breath like nerve gas, but for a minute, maybe two, there they were, dancing like lovers immortal, there was no getting around it. True love, they were up to their necks in it.

CRIMEWAVE
with
DEF FX
PUNTERS CLUB
Nov. 19th. A SUNDAY

JACK THE DANCER

Neil Boyack

JACK

It's the first night of your residency and you've taken them old Christmas cards out from your little brown baggie, cut them up for spliff filters, baby Jesus, Three Wise Men headin' for that star. The gear calms you down, cools you, so you can play hot on stage, the new easy listening sensation, makes you get inside them songs you play. Unzip the annexe and step inside to that fluffy purple floor and the orange lampshades and the numbered dancing couples lookin' like they came fresh out of their mummy's shute dancin' slow. Read the Christmas cards; lots of love Mum and Dad. And your Dad had a dose of Jack the Dancer when he died. You read the cards and smell new plastic life from inside the cards, plastic men

13

with plastic guns, plastic footballs destined for roofs with ratshit gutters, plastic hearts. And you sit for a second; then you start cutting, love Mum and Dad. Things you remember about your dad: that fluorescent cross in the front bedroom, a man who spoke in tongues around his house, drove that blue Kingswood into the ground, on doomed fishing trips, just to get away from the house, that pop-up house, kept castin' that line even when he ran out of bait, threw that line into the big brown river, loved the sound of that river, like a football crowd if he closed his eyes, stood near the tarred wood bridge, that was his spot, near the worn down campers' BBQ, he stood under one of the few trees, 360 degrees of wheat gold hills was all he could see. The water was so cold, like diving into chocolate ice-cream, sun was burnin', the odd snake going with the current, shape of an S. He was a large man who was balding, bearded man who believed that the end of the world was always near, believed in the power of the Lord, power of faith healers, signs from above. Married a woman three weeks after meeting her, they were doing the right thing there for the first month, things were shithouse from then on, ordinary for the next twenty years. But they were never in love, true love, Ray 4 Lucie 4 ever true love, never. He sat on a creaky fold-out chair on the cracked concrete verandah, watched the road out front turn from dirt to tar, picked his teeth with a match, blood on the match didn't change a thing, hoped for the world to start to end so he wouldn't have to mow those lawns. Nature strip was thick and dense with buttercups and weeds that didn't flower. Put a buttercup under your chin to see if you like butter, looked like no-one lived there after a while. Lucie pissed off across the road, couldn't stand his eating, his smell. His mate Jack the Dancer made him down and quiet. Still cooked him meals, and they watched TV together. They turned into friends just before he passed. She was nice to him, still had a photo of him somewhere, a happy snap from the week he went to Sunnyside, claimed he'd had a breakdown, voluntary admission. Cured after a week in Sunnyside, a week of sitting under beach umbrellas stuffed into bowling greens, eating cut lunches with lunatics who laughed at farts and cried when it rained. There was no conversation there, no debate, so he came back and watched as Lucie moved across the road to the basement space that was offered. She listened to water run through pipes, footsteps, all day looking at the roof. She faded out looking at that roof.

AFTER PARTY

The guests leave you leaning in a doorway. The show was good tonight, your first night, a good performance, everybody seemed to enjoy it. The guests have given you beer, wine, spirits, dope and conversations on why you were so good. There was talk of a recording deal, a new suit, an east coast tour, but you're trying to stay standing at the moment. Eyes close slowly, open sometimes. Leaning in a doorway, looking at green floor tiles. People walk past you to the ice machine on the fridge, pat you on the shoulder, saying great show tonight man, great show. You make a noise when they say that, give a half smile. And you look at the floor trying to work out where you are, where you can sit down, so you sit down there in the doorway of the kitchen and this old tune comes into your head from nowhere so you start to whisper it—Black Betty had a baby, bam ba lam, Black Betty had a baby, bam ba lam, damn thing was crazy, bam ba lam, damn thing was crazy, bam ba lam, Black Betty didn't mind, Black Betty didn't mind, damn thing was blind, damn thing was blind . . . You sit in this doorway whisperin' this tune, clappin' your hands soft.

SECOND NIGHT OF RESIDENCY

Now you got this new spliff up and running, it's a racer, feel the dull hoops of grass starting at your feet, rising all the way up past your blue eyes, disintegrating into dopey halos. Jack the guitar man, play your Country cocktail, showtime in two minutes. This time last month bottled off stage in some tin-pot pub. Prawn pink eyes, broken teeth, waking up in the backseat of your flat-tyre Falcon, some beach-side car park, sunrise through the windscreen gettin' in your eyes. But you're in the Duke room for the next fortnight because you called that number that you found scrawled on your hand. Couldn't remember how the hell it got there, who put it there, didn't know who it belonged to. It was almost worn off, thank Christ you didn't wash that week. You remember that week because there was nothing but the abandoned service station toilets; drank in them, shat in them, slept in them, dreamt truckin' diesel dreams, and there was the mosquitos. The 5-year-old calendar on the wall above the urinal. And you rang that number when you found one of them phonecards and you told the long distance voice that you were Jack. Turned out that you were speaking direct to the man who booked the talent for the casino, the Duke room. The voice talked fast, talked about how he saw you play a few tunes a couple of weeks back at this hotel that his little sister Lorna runs. Asks you if you remember the place.

THE PLACE

You were playing for your dinner that night, two light trucker drinking hole in the middle of the State. You remember some foul-mouthed lady lickin' your neck after the show, same dog-breath lifting her dress, putting herself in your mouth.

Yeah, I remember the place, you say. Remember going down on her 'cause she told you to. See, it was her birthday, she was the birthday girl. Next thing you're upstairs in her creaky bedroom and she has a hot clothes iron in her hand as she rides the stinkin' white horse, ironing the bedsheet next to your ear as old brown and grey family portraits hang there watching, handlebar-moustached goldminers.

Yeah, I remember the place, you tell him, you said Lorna didn't you? Yeah, I remember the place.

Remember waking up, iron on the floor next to the bed, scorched carpet, taking money off the dresser, taking three pairs of clean socks, listening to Lorna snore, a whistle in her nose, looking in a crooked mirror that was chained to the wall, getting the fuck out of there, ass hangin' out of pants.

But it's showtime now and someone in a red dinner suit is paid to introduce you so you take your instrument out of its case. Butterflies are always good before a show, normal. Swig your beer and walk onto the stage, hear your steps, polished floorboards, feel the warmth of the dull red lights, look to your right, can't see anything but lights. It's possible that there is no audience. As you take your jacket off, you can hear glasses clinking, small talk, cutlery noises, and they can see through the thin shirt, see the backyard tattoos, the markings, the faded stars, the tattered lost lovers up your forearms. They see the

17

eagle that looks like a puffin, that was your important, first tattoo. You got it up beside the high school library, got it in classtime, got it from Brett who held your arm like a fish. Brett had a cigarette hangin' from his mouth, Brett was expelled the year before. Brett looked at you through the smoke, squinted at your arm and cleared his throat. In the quick-flashing drags he bumsucked, you could hear the tobacco of his cigarette burn, watched it burn down past the brand name. And Brett kept sayin' it's all gonna' be worth it, it's comin' out real good, it's all gonna be OK 'cos you heated the point of that compass up real good with that lighter, heard the thing hiss in the green vegetable dye.

The young-smelling girls sit at the round tables near the stage. Red candles throw flickering light onto the high cheekbones, orange dots of lit cigarettes, blue light from above. The young girls are older than they make out. It's the smell of bubblegum that keeps them young, their whisper talk of being drunk. Chain smokin' bottle blondes that watch you with slanted heads, dreamy eyes as you sing.

SPARKTAIL FINGERS

And you'll be awake with her asleep on your chest, listening to the creak of a tin wind. Awake with the one who was nearest the stage, short haired, sockeyed, ice blonde. Said she's a dancer, out of work, she had a fat ring on each finger, they took the heat away from her plain face. And she moved her fingers to show you what she could do, and your eyes followed the flashes in the blue stage light, sparktail fingers. She watched your eyes watching her fingers. She's asleep now on your chest. The white light of a TV screen comes from the corner of the room, a tired car exhaust pops somewhere. It's this time of the morning you can hear the starting gates of the dog track clapping open, the lure rising and falling. Dog trials. Greyhounds can be seen with the binoculars, see their teeth, from the tenth floor balcony their loose tongues in their muzzles, their thick breath on cold mornings, their willingness, owners leading them, talking to them. Your hands are behind your head, the dancing rings asleep on your chest until you bring her out of her dreams of rusty autumn leaves. She wanted to stay there. You position her on top of you, she nods off as she takes you in, a distant crow in your breathing. That's the way. Your hands purchasing her soft hips, softest skin in the world. You want to keep touching, you get something out of just touching. She falls off sideways, leaves you there jacking off, sleeps with her head hanging off the edge of the bed. She'll tell her friend she fucked you, sucked you, they'll say WHO? Soon she wakes up, doesn't know who you are for a minute, Jack? Isn't it? You look to her handbag when her mobile phone rings. She answers it, someone tells her that her car has been burned out. She leaves without saying goodbye.

OLD GIRLFRIEND

Third night of your residency in the Duke room, you see an old girlfriend after the show. Fiona. She is with her new boyfriend and his friends. You talk for a few minutes. Pat your forehead with the back of your hand, still sweating from the show. So, what's happening? you ask. Oh nothing much she says. You see a lakeside holiday in her eyes, her family caravan, Chicken Kiev, off-peak, no-one to bother you except the last legs of a warm sun. Water skiing behind the boat she's driving, flying along flat blue water that reflects the sky, onshore pine trees, the deepest green. You can smell the cigarette she's holding when you lose your balance and skid along the water, into the water. She keeps going, adjusting her sunglasses, her bikini top, thinkin' of her mother's insomnia; cupboards squeaking in a dark kitchen. The outboard fades. You are there in the middle of the lake treading the dark water, waiting for her return. Then you ask her why she cut her hair, she says she doesn't really know, and then you ask her if she'll leave everything for you, she looks across to the boyfriend, who is looking at her. Butch has an unsettling crew cut. She smiles at him, turns back to you with a want, says, maybe as her mouth searches for an ouzo straw, misses it, gets it, sucks it, eyes flicking all over the place. Maybe she'll throw her new boyfriend away. She's thinking of how she can break it to him while you're telling her that you can both just go north to Byron Bay, leave everything. She's seeing Butch smashing the place up, seeing his chipped teeth close up, seeing Butch following her north, busting in on her while she's fucking. Her eyes focus on yours. There is a silence, like the bottom of the sea, waiting for her. Then you cut her off mid-sentence, you've changed your mind, you're going. See you around, you say to her. Fiona stands there looking. You turn and walk, expecting something heavy to hit you.

THE MANAGER'S ROOM

Crowd is good tonight. Mirror ball is moving slow, a hundred pin spots making ashtrays at the bar flare as slow as matches, smell of burning hair, a couple of blue lights on your face. The red velvet curtains billow behind you with the air-conditioning. Close the eyes when you sing up high while punters at the numbered tables smell the burning hair, push their fingers through their beautiful hair, ruining how they had it, go back to watching you close your eyes. That's how you do it for them, closing your eyes.

Thin Dali-moustache manager comes up to you after the show, used car salesman handshake, great show Jack great show. This is the man who booked you, pays you five grand like he's passing you a drink, rubs your arm, tells you there's some good fuck films going on upstairs, leaves the offer open when Lux comes in from the side somewhere while you're packing your guitar. Lux, queen sissy fag, start your eyes at his feet then rise to where the unlit cigarette is. Black native skin, a hint of fake tan even here. Cha-cha-cha. Lux says he's goin' up to the manager's room to watch those films, so you follow him holding your guitar case. Ten floors of elevator silence, four mirrors, gold carpet suits Lux's complexion you think. Lux does his lips in a compact mirror, starts gettin' funky, sort of feelin' himself up, starts hummin' a little ditty. Breathing through the nose, watch the numbers of the elevator reach the tenth floor. Lux is lovin' in the hope of being loved, done it all his life.

You leave the elevator, no-one but the two of you there, walk around corners, along carpet as quiet as sand, until you reach the manager's room. Before you sit anywhere, the manager wants to sing a song. He is holding a ginger-coloured drink, sings *Stand By Your Man* and Lux dances around the room like he can, like he coulda gone somewhere, but he's here in the dull yellow room, looking out on city lights with this old bloke singing.

YOUR NIGHT OFF

So it's your night off and you're sitting in front of the television. Big haired man in a camel-coloured suit narrates the re-enactment of a bank robbery. You have three Christmas cards left, you decide that you will cut into the nativity scene, the little light that comes from the manger, the centre of the whole picture. Joseph, Mary, Three Wise Men look on. Someone has drawn a number on the back of one of the Wise Men, an idolised football player, number 35. The Three Wise Men as running flankers. You roll Baby Jesus up gently and stuff him into one end of the joint. You light, you smoke, you look at the date on the Christmas card. Fifteen years old, the card is from your sisters. You realise that since Ray and Lucie have been gone, you haven't heard from them. They are distant relatives, they left home before you were a teenager. Love Cindy and Marie. You don't know where they are now. So you go back to the TV.

GREYHOUND RACERS

You go to the chemist that adjoins the casino, 6 p.m. You haven't been able to shake that sore throat. Tonight has been a sell-out, your last show here. You've got to get something for that sore throat, so you purchase some red medicine and you're leaving when they barge in, stuffing a gun into the chemist's forehead, he faints as one goes behind the counter, smashing the cash register, one stays on the door, one sees you, says you're dead mother-fucker, one says get him to drive. Then you're driving, faster asshole. Hit the Western Highway, hit the back of your head with their squeaking leather glove one inch punches. The three in the back seat stop panting, tell you to turn the radio on, not to look around or they'll blow your ugly head off. Radio plays *King of the Road*, they all sing along to it. Getting dark now, switch headlights on. Soon there are no more traffic lights, road gets a little thinner, no more streetlights, hobby farms. They snort something in the back seat. They're saying this is where it's at, then they drop out, and then you start slowing the car down, take your time to ease it up, from a hundred to nothing in five minutes, park it on the shoulder, keep it running, leave the purple door open, start jogging back the way you came. Hear your footsteps on the road, your red medicine back in the car, there are the crickets going now. You tug at your cuffs, touch your throat.

When the greyhound racers pick you up, they wipe the seat because you have a dinner suit on. She gets out of the passenger side, you get in between them, your arms touch them. The dashboard is dusty, gold cigarette packets from left to right, the windscreen wiper arches carved in dirt. They drive towards the glow of the city, can't see nothin' between their lights and the horizon. The interior light is on for some reason, dull like a nightlight. They have two dogs in the greyhound trailer, Hollywood and Ginger, they're racing tonight. This is a big meeting, a city meeting, the top dogs will be racing, the prize money is good. The radio in the car is down low, same station as the getaway car, *By the Time I Get to Phoenix*. To your left she has a pink jumper, pink lippy, name like Darl, heart of gold. To your right, the driver has a tan wrinkled face, like a satellite photograph of a river delta, one of those faces that looks unshaven regardless. Gold pack of Virginia stickin' up out of his body shirt top pocket, he turns the radio up, looks across to his wife, says they're playing our song Darl. He tells me he's been racing dogs for years, tells me he likes cars, used to drive buses for a living. He looks out to his right, he sees a house set back on a block, the solitary porch light of the house, goes back to looking at the yellow headlights on the road, tells me about Judy. She won everything, he says, taking his hands off the wheel, didn't she Darl? She makes a noise, he's tapping the wheel, he starts singing *Green Green Grass of Home*, starts coughing up blood onto the wheel, coughs for a kilometre, coughs less and less until he stops. Three, two, one. We all look at the blood on the Holden lion and he keeps smoking because he knows he has to. And then she needs to go, so he pulls onto the shoulder of the highway. By this time you are approaching the outskirts of the city, the streetlights are appearing. The car idles as slow as a heart.

'Tourists, man. ~~They just~~ I swear they
sprinkle-bags full of ~~pubes~~
~~their~~ pubes before the
close the door.'
                    — Portland Lodge
                        employee.

'I hate ~~them~~ the furry little
fuckers, shitting everywhere,
~~always going~~ ~~piss~~ ~~scratch~~
head-butting the walls.'
                    — Portland Hotel
                        employee.

                    get up!
'Bobby, you're sitting on the
china man.'   Men's dormitory.

                                    Look.
                        'The feral scrubbers'
                    off to another root.'

                    'Come on. Let's all go for
                    a jetty jump.'
                                        Beth

                    'Sam's somersaulting on
                    the beach again.'

                    'Taxi!'

                            Whenever a door
                            glass breaks.

                    'What wanker pissed on
                    my towel?'

                    'Looked good. Sea
                    professional.'

                            — After Eileen
                            stacked her bike

            ~~Where's the~~

            'I've been here too long.
            hey.

                        little
            'Who's the dude sleeping
            in ~~my~~ my room?'
            'Dunno. ~~Who's he~~ ~~about~~
            ~~there I don't~~ Isn't he with
            ~~my friend not~~ you?'

SMALL BOY FALLING

Glyn Parry

Harry has seen her again. The horny one who plays worn down Donna Summer records whenever her man is away. The slutty one who boasts about the photo she secretly sent to 'Rosie' magazine. He says he wants to rescue her from a life of domesticity. I ask him to phone back.

'Don't wanna know, hey, big brother? You born-agains got no idea.'

I groan. Harry isn't about to hang up.

'She's kept her looks. Beautiful tits considering how many kids she's had. Babes been bugging me any-hows.'

I lean into my desk. Harry picks the worst time to talk dirty.

'Met her on Rottnest Island. Remember Rotto, big

brother? Schoolies week? Stealing the pushies? God'll get ya. He's gonna send you to the other place.'

'Harry, look—'

'Was it you or your retard mate who killed the quokka?'

'Harry, I have a—'

'Met her on the beach. In front of the beer garden. Some cunt reckoned Mick Jaggers were going down, but I never scored any.' He laughs that donkey laugh of his. 'Had the travel bug all summer, hey.'

He'll phone the surgery anytime about anything. At Christmas it was that Dana Point mafia thing. What was it he called Slater? A gerbil-shoving jerk.

'We got Supertubes! We got Lefthanders! Anyhows, seppo jerks got jack shit!'

Strange rumblings. I asked him where he was phoning from.

'Work. The chicken place.'

Last Easter it was the wrecking yard. He said he was chucking it in to follow the sun around the planet. Said alls he ever wanted was an endless summer.

'As in that movie?'

'As in stuff you and your round-bellied gangster molls, big brother. Get a life before they dump you in frozen goods.'

I am part of the conspiracy. It's what he thinks. There's no escaping my baby brother's insecurity. For my house-warming he rented *The Stepford Wives* and played the final supermarket scene over and over. He thinks I sold out.

'That's you, big brother. That's you if you don't get your shit together. Doctor Dolittle. Ker-ching, ker-ching. Hear them dollars fall.'

It's these Saturday morning phone calls that get me the most.

Today I listen anyway. Maybe it's the tone of his voice.

'Hubby's a truckie. Retard mongrel. Doesn't pay her enough attention.'

Or maybe it's Lesley Carrington sitting so close.

'Anyhows, she's got a thing for young blokes. You should see the scratch marks.'

I want to tell Harry he's skating on thin ice, like all the other times. Married women are a mistake.

He snorts, carries on.

'Guess what?'

I sigh. There are other patients to see. Always other patients to see. It's my job. It's what I do.

'They found the *Titanic*.'

I laugh too readily. 'That's old. Everyone knows that already.'

'No kidding!' Harry's voice, all crackle and pop. 'I only just heard. Mate, when she goes down on me, hey.'

I don't want to know. About his hell summer on Rottnest Island. About the cones he pulled, the bad poetry he endured, all the 19 year olds he woke up next to. I don't want to know about this deluded woman playing 'Hot Stuff' and 'Bad Girls' while the littlies sleep in the next room, but Harry tells me anyway.

'Is that traffic I hear?'

'Could be, big brother. What ya doing for the week-end?'

'You know exactly what I'm doing. Keeping my promise.'

'I mean tonight, dickhead.'

Before I can answer he tells me about the black-and-white surf videos they projected onto the wall of the saloon bar.

'Has-been surfers and that shit new pommy band. All the sunburnt Jergens from Sweden loved it. Rotto goes off, hey.'

How can I tell him I had tickets to see that shit new pommy band?

And then, when I am least expecting it, 'Be ruthless, big brother. Bury the bitch. Stop making promises anyhows.'

Harry hangs up.

The bitch is my mother. Last week she called twice. I emptied thin assurances onto the line, emptied myself. I have no need of her voice. It has no past, only clutter. It's what I pretend.

One night I crept into my parents' room to stand at the foot of their bed, hoping to make her go away, disappear, scat, don't come back. She stirred, caught me looking down on her. I said nothing. Dad slept. He always slept.

I compose myself. Lesley Carrington has listened to every word.

'My brother, Harry. You remember Harry?'

She bites her bottom lip the way some women do, teeth white with prosperity. I think, Can she be playing with me after so long?

'There's a screen behind you.'

She smiles and moves away. I study her card. I try not to listen to the rustle of clothes, to imagine silk panties, to encourage a hard-on. Ha.

Carrington.

She has kept her maiden name and I know precisely the last time I heard it.

I was down from uni. Harry still lived in Bunbury then. He had his licence and—after an afternoon's drinking at Caves House, Yallingup—wanted to show me some wild place down south he had discovered on a surfing binge. Contos Field. We pulled into Caves Road, drove past the wineries and galleries, past the Gracetown and Prevelly turn-offs, past Mammoth Cave and the start of the karri forest.

It was dark before we even got there.

'Look for the Lake Cave entrance,' said Harry.

All I saw was twisted branches and an owl leap into silent flight. I shouldn't have had that last beer. Should've gone for a swim instead, or soaked up rolling lawn, or watched another crummy sunset. The karri forest is full of ghosts.

He got onto the right track. Branches straightened out and I saw stars once more. Someone sprinted naked past the front of the XC into the bush and Harry hooted, fist pounding the car horn.

'Weird fucken kangaroos, hey!' He fired off an imaginary round.

I drifted past in a haze of alcohol. In the next clearing blazed a bonfire. Parking was tight. Harry inched forward at a difficult angle and the XC almost side-swiped the panel van with the faded seventies dragon painted on its side. When he pulled on the handbrake the dragon mushroomed into a tangle of blonde hair and loud abuse.

'Light years away, retard!' Harry didn't care.

I laughed and kicked open the passenger door. 'Hey, mate, got any munchies?' I didn't care, either.

Somewhere nearby rose the cooo-eee cry of a party

animal. My baby brother trampled long grass and headed for the fire.

'Harry!'

He pointed to the rising moon and kept on walking.

'Hey there, stranger.'

The voice turned me around and I almost fell. A girl I vaguely knew. She lifted a UDL can to her mouth.

'You remember me?'

I nodded, swayed.

'Liar.' She stepped forward and pushed the warm can to my mouth.

'Lesley Carrington's little sister. Youth camp, remember? Me and my friend put toothpaste on your windscreen.'

'God, yeah. You've grown.'

'Aw, duh.' She headed back to the others.

'Got anything to eat?'

She said something. I tried to hear. The grass was long and she faded away.

Carrington.

Now I realise her older sister has been speaking to me, stepping out from behind the screen.

'Sorry?'

'I said I heard he got himself into some sort of trouble.'

'Oh, that was nothing.' I put her card down. 'He's renting a caravan now. Kwinana. He's right on top of the industrial stuff, but he's not complaining. Goes down south often enough. Stops in here.'

But I don't want to talk about Harry.

'Well, let's have a look at you.'

The years fall away. I hear the thunder of traffic biting down hard on bitumen. I taste dust and raw courage. The first attempt was at youth camp. We dismissed the sing-along, the supper, quiet time. We were good Baptists. Somewhere in the middle of it all a tourist coach hummed, roared, threw handfuls of gravel at my clumsy efforts. The grass itched. I burned. After she ran back to the girls' dorm I leaned my ear to the peppermint tree to hear Satan's laughter trickle up from the sand.

'Just relax.' I proceed with the examination. 'Let's see what we're dealing with first.'

'Maybe I should cut the weekend short.' She pulls her legs up, parts her thighs. 'You know, the spotting. But I don't want to drive all the way back to Perth and find it's nothing.'

I ask her where she is headed and she tells me she has the use of a beachfront cottage in Dunsborough.

'I like to get away. I like the freedom.'

I feel her watching me the whole time. Her belly curves and I ache to follow. I want to fall into her voice. She talks about the baby's room back in Claremont. I know she is trying to impress me. I wonder if she is married, separated, divorced, widowed. She only talks about herself, her things and the baby. I dare not think of her all alone.

We go quiet. I guide my fingers between swollen lips, do what I'm paid to do. She gasps, so quietly that I almost miss it. After this the morning will pass slowly. No idle chatter. No small talk. Just pills and prods and casual glances of the body.

'Does that hurt?'

She says nothing. When I look up she smiles and shakes her head.

'There?'

'Nope.'

I wish Harry hadn't phoned. I wish Bunbury didn't have to be this eternal stopover for neurotic surfers and rich bitch women.

'Long time no see,' I say, finishing up. And almost die.

'It's okay. I know what you mean.'

I ask her if she still goes to church.

'Not since high school. And you?'

I shake my head. She seems saddened by that.

After work I see the old Holden in the driveway and groan. Harry waits for me on the verandah. My house looks tired in the heat, walls baked hard and paint peeling like old men crying. He is slumped in the lazy chair, looking up the street. He has his surfboard and gear with him.

'Where ya bin?'

'Stopped at the deli. Needed some things.'

'Government's threatening to fuck up the dole again.'

'Oh, Harry . . . '

Somewhere outback there is a garage with Harry's name painted on the side. The real Harry, all covered in oil and singing loud anthems beneath the bonnets of dusty autos. Not this whingeing defeatist attitude baby brother of mine.

We walk inside to escape the heat. His leg rope trails across the floor. The hallway has just been polished.

'Put your stuff away. Then tell me more sordid details about this married woman.'

Until just after Christmas Harry dismantled car wrecks on the sly in some hot shed near the freeway. Social Security didn't need to know. There was a different married woman back then.

After much dirty talk he says, 'Wanna go to Traffs tonight?'

Now I know he is in a dangerous mood. We go there sometimes. One time we got loud. Harry wasn't listening. I told him about Kwinana's polluted water, about not eating any seafood caught locally.

'Come back to Bunbury,' I said, topping up his glass. 'They got rid of the silo. The BP tanks are gone.'

That was the night he told me about the stripper.

'Bulldust! Where?'

'Top of Lesmurdie Hill. Below the water tower. Reckoned she was into water sports, hey. So what if I let her do it? Fucked me senseless anyhows.'

We were shouting, laughing, spilling our drinks. Harry grabbed me by the shirt, kissed me. We were a lost cause that night. Punters watched our crazy dance. Some grinned. Others went back to their beers.

'Tonight. Just you and me. What d'ya say, big brother? Supertubes can wait.'

'Maybe.' I send him down the passageway to the bathroom. It's been a hot drive down and Harry sweats easily.

An hour later we eat at Hungry Jack's. Six years out of uni and I'm still eating the same junk food, still envying the same fast cars.

They could knock the whole town down, I want to say. Bunbury won't ever change.

Instead I tell him what's been on my mind since morning.

Harry looks impressed.

'I wanted to, you know . . . ' I stumble on. Where am I? Why am I telling Harry all this? I'm the respectable one.

My baby brother looks at me real close. I forget how cruel he can be. He says things about Lesley Carrington I could never have known.

'When?'

'You were in Perth. At uni. Anyway, I give her a go meself. We all did. Back at Robbo's place.'

I want to leave. I want to smash the movie tie-in glass on the table and stab Harry in the face. How could I have fallen for a whore like Lesley Carrington?

'Sorry, brother. Thought you knew.'

My mind spins. We eat slowly. I wonder if the day is ruined already. I wonder if I should go home. Only, Harry wants to go for a swim. In the river.

'What river?'

First we go next door to grab a birthday present before the shops close. Big W. Harry walks over to the music section when I look like spending too long.

'Found anything?' He's back. Bored already. What money is there for CDs when you're on the dole?

'I don't know any more.' I am desperate. 'You choose.'

'With pleasure.' He sprints away, meets me back at the checkouts two minutes later. His life is a slingshot.

'What is it?'

'Some teddy bear cross-stitch thing.'

'Will she like it?'

'Dunno.'

'Will she be able to do it?'

'Does it matter?'

My scheming mother. Birthdays are an affirmation of loyalty. Harry hasn't talked to her since the funeral. It means I'm the one she attacks.

'They change.' I fish out my Mastercard and hand it over. 'When one goes, the other withdraws. Or grows cranky. Or sees only flaws.'

Harry says nothing. He's hardly even talked about her since the funeral. Tomorrow her bitterness will search me out. She will be powerful and dangerous, her words like running blades, and this is the best I can give her?

The checkout operator wants my signature.

My meticulous signature, littering exercise books and stories and projects stretching back into my high school years. She keeps everything, my mother.

'Should have bought her a box of chocolates,' I say afterwards, tossing the package into the back seat of Harry's Holden.

'They'd melt, big brother.'

We take the Old Coast Road out of Bunbury. I listen to the slick sound of the new FM station. More prizes. More give-aways. *Too* slick.

'I bet you're glad you don't have to listen to this crap every day.' My turn to be bored. 'At least you get Triple J.'

But he isn't listening. He's remembering. Wants to show me the tree where he gouged out his own meticulous signature. And the river. His stories bring the river to life. I am curious to see.

'Best time of day.' He means the sun, the heat.

'Just don't get us bogged.' Clean air rushes in and I try to forget tomorrow.

'Seen the horses?' He points. The sun glances off hills.

'You wish.'

I hear him sigh as we approach the Australind turn-off,

like he wants to shed tired skin. I'd forgotten how much this place means to him.

Harry's place.

We are suddenly there, past clumps of trees. There beside the river. Wild ducks rise and disappear. Bush crowds in. Sickly gums stain the sky.

'Wanna skinny-dip? No-one's around.'

I don't answer.

'Gutless.' He switches off the ignition.

Summer grass falls in long shadows. Tall spears sway.

'Further up they use this place to dump car bodies.' He shrugs his wide shoulders. 'This whole stretch is like a giant graveyard for cars. They've even got cars in the river.'

He surveys landmarks from his youth. It isn't difficult to imagine a bunch of kids claiming a place like this for their own.

'Through there's the mudflats. That's where we rode our trail bikes. So ya going in or what?'

This water is not like the ocean. I think of leeches and broken glass. I think of Ross River virus. I wind my window up to keep out the flies and mozzies.

'But it looks so dirty.'

'Just muddy. Right there's where the feral woman jumped in.' He points upstream to the sharpest bend.

'And you never found out who she was?'

'Nah. She was right out of it. Swam across. Took off into the bush, shouting and bleeding.'

The river jumps. I join its madness.

Definitely Harry's place.

'And over there?'

'Yep, I guess we're all in there, some place or other.'

I look to the far bank. The narrow island. Their

private coastline. So easy to be consumed, to ambush, to hide. They took their aim. They fired their first shots and hid.

'Is that the rope?' My foolish question.

'Probably. You wouldn't read about it.'

The long rope falls from the overhanging limb, its knotted end measured to adolescence. Their rope, abandoned now. I wonder when he first dared to push off from the bank, to surrender fully to the rope and the wide circle it made.

'Weren't you scared of drowning? Anything could've happened.'

'Hell, no. Too busy getting shit-faced.'

I picture him drunk and stoned, sailing out over the deep channel, laughing loud, letting go.

'Pity you all lost contact.'

'That bunch of fuckwits? No way.'

'I wonder what happened,' I say finally. I am studying that bend in the river.

'That silly feral? Forget her.'

'But who was she? Why was she shouting?'

'Shit happens.' Harry unfastens his seatbelt and climbs into sunshine.

I watch him undress. Afternoon shadows drape across his flesh. His body shows no sign of slipping. He makes sure of that. His one great belief is the body.

He leaves his things on the bonnet and walks to the water's edge. Waves once, then drops down into brown water. His feet kick powerfully.

'Be careful,' I say. Sometimes I only say things as an afterthought.

Harry glides just below the surface. He takes a lungful of air, pushes on. A trail of small bubbles follows him to the other side. I see him pull himself out, hands grasping heavy tree roots. Soon he is seated comfortably on the other bank, in the shade of a tree.

Their tree.

He looks well pleased with himself when he finds his initials and I know he is mocking the world. There's something spiteful about boys being boys, sharp blade passing from hand to hand.

I am still looking for answers when Harry seizes the rope and launches himself. He wears a maniac's grin. Drops like stone.

And now it is evening. Traffs has turned wanky since Harry's last visit. The place stinks of new money.

'Okay, so educate me.' I cannot believe we are discussing the merits of hitting the chemical trail.

'One. It's cheap. Gotta go to Goa, hey. Just don't spend your fare home. Two. It's got beaches and babes.'

'I thought you said babes were bugging you.'

'Hey, fuck you.' Harry gulps down his drink. 'Three. Australia's rooted. The Keating days are over.'

'Tell me more about that feral woman.' I swing the topic away from politics. 'Where'd she come from?'

My baby brother leans in close. 'We found her canoe, right? Half-sunk in the mud and shit.'

'Yeah. So?'

'So we trashed it, right? I said we should hang on to it. You know, salvage rights and all, but my mates were too shit-faced.'

'So you trashed it?'

'We sank it, yeah. Just like the *Titanic*.'

'And the woman?'

'Well, it was like I said. She jumped in and swam to the other bank.'

'Upstream?'

'Yeah. Upstream. Like I told you.' Now it's Harry's turn to change topics. 'I'm still doing me research on them A-bomb tests. Bastards.'

Harry blames Dad's death on the first British atomic bomb tests on Christmas Island back in the fifties.

'They nuked the old man. No shit. Anyone standing above decks got sunburnt. You've seen the slide.'

One black-and-white slide, scratched to insignificance in a box under the bed in my mother's new unit.

'He's gone, Harry. You have to let go.' I say this as gently as I can.

'Fucken pommy government. As bad as the Americans.' Harry leans even closer. 'Seen the greasy cunt behind you? Used to be my Maths teacher.'

After a couple more beers, and disapproving looks, we go to the Burlington. A rough pub, as rough as they come.

Outside, half a dozen Harleys take up two parking bays. A blue heeler has its chain stuck under its owner's ute. An impossibly tall Aboriginal man leans against brickwork and smokes. I think of jackaroos. I like the romance the image brings.

Inside, the sound check fills one corner. I buy the first round, the second, the third. It is an evening for pool cues and posturing. Bon Jovi's 'Blaze of Glory' has one of the bikers serenading. Someone breaks a plate out the back. 'Taxi!' roars the table closest to the kitchen. I am bored already.

Not Harry. He's been in a funny mood since bumping into his old sawmill boss. Up the end of the bar former workmates ignore him. Someone lost a finger and Harry got the sack for not following safety procedures. Old poisons run close to the surface of his skin.

I think, If he picks a fight I'm leaving.

But there is no fight. Harry stares across the crowded bar, his gaze dropping off the edge of the world. The girl has been staring. She's wearing one of those tight-fitting numbers older women hate. The river of her perfect body carries his venom out to sea.

Until the boyfriend turns up with drinks and catches my eye. They both do. I look away a moment too late.

'This place is rooted, hey.' Harry turns back to me, turns his back on them all.

'We can go home. Get a video on the way.'

Only, Harry sees someone else. He slides off his stool and rushes over to where the band eternally sets up.

'Bloody Spider McPhee!'

Another mate, this one up from Bridgetown. I shake the clammy hand. They're buried in there. In from the bush. Or out on parole. I forget how popular Harry is.

After an eternity the band starts up, a cover of Iggy Pop's 'Lust for Life', and I'm almost impressed. Then I remember *Trainspotting* and feel ripped off.

A girl spirals onto the dance floor, arms outstretched like an aeroplane. At the bar, raw men pause mid-sentence to have a look-see. But she is nothing, this wild child. A bush pig, as my baby brother would say. Shooter of the month. Black Death.

Jesus, how can I even think these things?

Another girl steps forward. Now there are two aeroplanes. Ha. I am drunk already. Girls dance with girls. Harry has left me for another man. Ha ha. I'm fucked.

That's when they make their move. The couple up the far end. Nice 'n' sleazy does it. I've seen this movie. I wonder if there are bodies trapped in the car wrecks at the bottom of the river? Do turtles play in the sunken canoe?

'You'll be right, mate.'

I try to forget our old house on the hill. The radio was different back then. DJs talked more. Songs stayed in the charts longer. All through summer Surfcats scratched the sky. I could never have sold up. Not that house there. Not for a unit in the middle of suburbia.

'It's good shit, hey.'

My father was thin and his lungs rattled. Even then he defended her. Now Harry hates her. Me, I hate only the wasted years.

'Through there, mate.'

I try to forget the sad woman losing her mind near the river. What branches keep her awake at night, scratching, scratching?

Paranoia catches me out. Doubts creep in. The tingle won't come. It is what I think in the alley, moments into my trip.

'Swallow or suck. Your call, mate.'

The girl is in my face again. She swings away, swings back, a convolution of colour. I think her face is melting.

'Just don't stay where the cops'll find you,' says her man.

I must be tripping. Suddenly I see so clearly. A woman all alone. Her drifting canoe. Lost boys all together. A knife.

'Oh, Harry . . .'

And now later, in the toilets, I watch a flotilla of canoes drift past their island. I *think* they are canoes, unless they are ghosts. I feel large and lazy like the river. I wish I wish I. The canoes have eyes. I wish I could take a piss. The mirror has eyes. What mirror? Oh.

The second attempt, my last, was on the grass at Meelup Beach. The moon was over everything. Her breasts. The flat of her stomach. She pushed her body into the cup of my hand and the clumsiness was all mine.

Weird, hey, the way everything crystallises into one perfect revelation. I messed up majorly with Lesley Carrington. So why track me down to my life of respectability and common sense?

How wide my eyes appear, staring back at me in the mirror.

'So they already found the *Titanic*?' Harry spies the bottom of his glass. 'Who gives a flying fart anyhows?'

I'm back. I think I'm back. Harry's trying not to make a scene. Spider McPhee humours him.

'Fucken cunts! All of them, hey! Jumped up fucken cunts!'

Harry's in no mood to be humoured.

I watch the dance floor and think of Lesley Carrington stepping naked from her Dunsborough cottage into the middle of the road. She turns in a slow circle, the soles of her feet warming to their own aeroplane dance. Grinning crocodiles have attached themselves to the cat's eye road markers. Ha ha ha. In one hand she holds out a small dead snake. No, not a snake. In the other she offers a foetus. Sometimes my paranoia leads to the strangest revelations. It is late, close to midnight, and I am thinking I would like to eat her. I am thinking I would like to have her in the back of Harry's Holden. Or run her down.

Harry is on his feet, shouting more obscenities. I jump. His voice is a storm raging in the noise and darkness. I'd help Spider McPhee pull him back down, but I'm next to useless. We are all very drunk. I'm definitely tripping.

'Let's go!' I shout. 'Let's go let's just yeah let's split now go fuck I'm fucked hey let's fucking go.'

Already I can see where it might end. Harry is dangerous when he roars like that. Even in the shadows he is dangerous. I look at Spider McPhee, but his eyes are fixed to the coloured lights. What does he care? The night never ends.

'It's late!'

Harry roars again. He tells me to shut the fuck up, big brother. Says buy another round. But what can he know? The dust is in her pores. Her body grinds favours for life. God save me from that whore Lesley Carrington.

Harry leaps to his feet again. The arc of his fist swings wildly, but he grins like a kid and falls back into his corner.

'We're going!' Now Spider McPhee is on his feet. Harry gets up beside him.

'Where to?'

'Dunno!' Harry yells in my face. 'But this place is rooted!'

I follow. I judge the narrow corridor, the couple coming the other way. We are out on the pavement again and the night air brings me down. Harry leads the way. He is drunk and loud and full of menace. He trips. A cop car slows down beside us, but moves on when Harry finds his feet again.

'It's late!' I shout. 'Let's go home, Harry!'

Harry and his mate dance. I see the vortex their

bodies make as they join and rejoin at the waist. I feel the atomic boom as they split the Burlington in two. They weave past Harleys, past fenders. The whole world is turning aeroplane.

'Play time, big brother!'

I slow down. There is a song. I slide down. There is a song on the radio that takes me back to the bitumen and the bay. She wanted to feel me pressing down against her, panting for her, kicking clutter aside. Her flesh wanted to shout for me, breasts come to life for me. I should have tightened my body against her. Scared her. Taken control. But I was just another good Baptist lacking imagination.

A shit song.

I stop. I crash. Harry and his mate both look foolish on their narrow island of noise. There are those coloured bulbs again. They burn the sky. I stop to shake out the demons, to cut loose the memory of ferals, bitches, whores. They are mad, I convince myself. Every woman is mad.

'Harry, wait.'

He ignores me. He didn't have the guts to leave me before, but now that it is late and madness fills the air, my baby brother leaves me to go nightclubbing. I'm left behind, a small boy falling. But I cannot follow.

✺ Maison Bob ✺

Mini Quiche with Chef's Fingernails
and Pan-Fried Toads

— 13.50

Boy-Flesh Baguettes au Citronne

—19.50

Frog's Spawn Vinaigrette

— 17.50

Terrine de Garden Snail

— 21.50

Fresh Leaf Salad

— 18.50

with cod's eyes   — 22.50

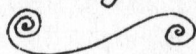

HARBOUR BRIDGE

Kathleen Stewart

The satisfying chink of china as he slung the saucers down in a line, resting on one another. And then the cups, their thick white ears aligned. Ben rubbed the chrome surrounds of the espresso machine absently with his tea-towel, smiling to himself, then remembered. The punters didn't want to see him, pimples and sweat, and oozing burns. He had a row of burns, from the griller, across the knuckles of his right hand, scabbed over, but never quite healing, always too wet—burns weeping into the dishwater—and another row across his left hand, like Nick's tattoos, h-a-t-e on one set of fingers and l-o-v-e on the other.

With his hate hand, Ben pushed his hair back from his forehead. He squinted, scanned the room, then rushed back into the narrow kitchen, where smoke was starting to rise from the grill. He pulled the tray out, burning the sides of his hands, swearing to himself. This was only the beginning of his shift, only the first of innumerable baguettes, the cups and saucers and plates coming in in an endless tide, and there was still room to burn on both hands.

Later, his hands moving frantically under water, his hair flipping back off his forehead as he tossed his head and sniffed, he thought, If I had a dog I could do something with all the bloody baguettes that go to waste.

He thought about all the painstakingly hand-layered salads, that no-one ever ate, that ended up adding a bit of colour to the table while they burbled on about their fucking salaries over the cabernets and the merlots and the imported beers. God, it's a poncy place, he thought. And for you, Madam, the lard tart? Or the pig's knockers? Double double decaf, not a flicker of a smile. All the food just window-dressing, decoy, blotting paper to soak up the drink, or something to do with the licence. Caviar in a bed of oakleaf lettuce, black olive pâté, marinated this and that; little bits of slime, served with rounds of toasted baguette. Slimy was the operative word. He imagined his father's face, his head pulled back into his neck as if he was trying to escape his body, his mouth puckered like a cat's bum. And his mum, looking sideways. They'd only just braced themselves to try *pizza*, for Christ's sake.

But mostly it was dishes, a mountain of dishes, never-diminishing, like a task set by a bad-tempered troll. Cups and saucers, saucers and cups, sticky, pink-smeared with lipstick, and blackened with coffee dregs. And him, with his hands underwater, fishing about for forks and knives, dishing plates from the suds into the rinse water, like so many thick white frisbees. Ben, who, as his mother pointed out, wouldn't be caught dead with his hands in dishwater ordinarily.

'Cups. I need cups,' shouted Nick. He put his big head round the corner. 'Hey, Stonewash! Having a snooze?'

Ben heaved another tray of cups out to the espresso machine, and stacked them quickly, while Nick sneered at him, his arms folded, his muscular gut thrust forward.

Over by the toilets, almost girlish with animation, Bob, the boss, was explaining something to a glaze-eyed bloke in a black suit. He looked across at Ben and Nick and his face closed. His mouth pursed, and his finely plucked eyebrows went up a fraction. There wasn't much room on his forehead. Ben grinned, and nodded, and whipped himself back out to the kitchen.

Bob owned a chain of S & M clubs, as well as this bar. The sick old fuck, thought Ben. Pathetic old geezers in vinyl, he thought, swinging plastic chains.

'Strictly speaking, I shouldn't be employing you, kid,' Bob had said, wrapping up a surprisingly short interview. 'But I believe in extending the hand of friendship to the younger generation. Stay in the kitchen. No smoking, of course. No fraternising with the clients. No nattering with the bar staff. Follow the menu. You'll be right.' A horrible wink.

Bob's horrible winks made Ben feel okay about slipping himself the odd extra fifty from the till. Danger money. Or something.

Another baguette, beginning to burn ever so slightly under the griller, another baguette served with a hint of boy-skin. This time it was the little finger on his love hand. Well, it was a job. And the time went surprisingly quickly, juggling the plates underwater, sliding from the fridge to the griller and back. And it wasn't cooking, really, just heating things up and arranging things on plates, and of course, dishes coming out of his arse, and the burns never healing, but he wasn't going to wear the gloves because they stank . . .

On his break, Ben smoked Winfield Blues, and thought about the dog he'd get one day, a rusty red cattle dog. He thought about Nick's tats, and were they painful to get, despite being done by the top man in Sydney?

Nick was cool, but humourless. One time, one lousy time, he'd worn his stonewash jeans into work. 'Hey, Stonewash,' Nick said. Like it was some big, cool joke. Now, it was, 'How you going, Stonewash?' Stonewash this, Stonewash that. There were all sorts of dress rules here that didn't apply at home. He'd had to get his mum to stop ironing creases into things. And, after all the trouble of getting them to pay for the haircut, now he had to grow the thing out.

When he was older—in two years he'd have his licence—he'd be like Nick. He'd wear his hair like that. He'd pour the drinks with a deft flick of the wrist, and a twist at the end that cut the liquid off with a snap you could almost hear. He'd buy himself a leather jacket, and he'd ride a hog, like Nick's.

Of course, Nick was a fake. Just like Bob and his friends in their little rubber suits were fakes. And *he* was a fake now. Which was probably why Nick kept on calling him Stonewash. To let him know he knew. And all the customers, miserable little would-be yuppies, sinking their smug noses into their bouquets of wine and eating their Mexican worms, were fakes. The trick was to be a good fake, to make sure that what you were going to pretend to be was a worthy choice.

He was taking another tray of cups out to the bar when he saw them—perched on the tiny silver stools that were shaped like a set of cheeks and a crack, in reverse. The pair of them, blonde, pale, sparkling, wearing cara-mel-coloured clothes. God, it was like the Great Gatsby. Robert Redford and Mia Farrow, but without the freckles. The woman lifted her champagne flute to him in a gesture of salute—was he gaping?—and smiled, her eyes shining, her fingers flashing jewels, even her fingernails gleaming, pink and clean. He turned on his heels, hurried back into the kitchen and stood by the sink, shy and breathless, and wide-eyed as a rabbit.

That was the first time that he saw them.

They were always together. Always dressed in pale, soft clothes. Always gleaming, with their shiny blonde hair, and their matching skin—pale and uniform as a pigskin wallet he'd once seen. And they held themselves high, like a pair of racehorses, laughing and smiling at each other, having a good time with each other, and never drunk and loud, like the others. From another planet.

I bet they have a dog, Ben thought. A tan labrador.

He thought of his mother and father. The way they had of sitting turned away from each other, not so you could mention it, not that you mentioned anything; just a shoulder here, a chin there. The way they flicked through their magazines, with the telly on already, flick, flick, busy impatient fingers, but it was just a way of letting a little irritation into the air. His father's face, grey and lined and sour, and his mother's, yellowing and creased as the paper bags she kept stuffed in the kitchen drawers.

Meanwhile, they leaned in their usual spot on the swivelling silver seats at the far end of the bar, laughing and smiling like a couple in a catalogue. Her fingers poised, like a woman in a commercial. Tipping her head back to laugh, a thin gold chain showing beneath her cream blouse. And his body turned towards her, attentive. Bending to murmur something witty in her ear. Flicking the gold lighter open, cupping his hand at her cigarette . . .

He remembered where he was. Twelve bloody baguettes, and Bob's griller only fitted five, and even then you had to juggle them about. He flicked the burnt edges onto the floor with a knife, blew off the char-dust, sliced them briskly, and lay them on their napkins, beside the slices of salmon, and the tiny dishes of so-called caviar, then slid the plates onto the counter and rang the bell.

Bob preferred girls to serve. Tarty girls in high-rise skirts, who only came into the kitchen to bot a cigarette, and pick up and drop off plates. He wasn't interested in them, and they weren't interested in him. He was the kitchen boy, the kid. Everyone called him Kid—except Nick, who stuck with Stonewash—and watched the red rise up his neck, deepening his pimples to cherry red. 'Kid,' said Bob, one night, possibly drunk. 'You have flair. My next place, I'm going to get a real kitchen. And you, Kid, are going to be my chef.' Which was a nice thought. But hadn't he noticed the burns?

For a few weeks, they didn't show. And then, when he watched the TV, alone in the loungeroom after his shift, he saw a women with pale-coloured pants, weeding a garden, advertising incontinence pads, and he thought of *her*. He saw an ad for a holiday, and he thought, I bet they ski. I bet they go to Aspen. Wherever that is. And when he saw a family with a dog, he thought, *They're* like that. Only happier.

At Christmas, staring in a trance at the metal tree— so that his mother said, 'You haven't guessed your present, have you?'—he saw them, sitting on a soft rug, while hundreds of pearl-sheen baubles danced on the pine branches above them. They were gazing at one another,

her head tilted back, his smiling face bent towards hers. The labrador would be rolling on its back, getting its stomach tickled. For a minute, his heart squeezed tight with jealousy. Then he leapt up. 'Time for bed,' he said.

'Night, night,' lisped his mother, her teeth already out.

His father grunted.

Ben lay in bed, and thought. His mother, for instance. His mother was not maternal. She cooked and she ironed and she did all the things she was supposed to do. She was like an alien who'd landed on earth and taught herself human from old American sitcoms. She was like Beaver's mum, without the smile. She hoovered and washed up and dusted, stern and grim as a foundry worker. Good boy, she said, and stiffly patted him on the head. Like she'd watched Lassie. Give your mum a kiss, she'd say, and turn her cheek towards him, hard as a plate. There, there, she said. Night, night. At the appropriate times. Stiff and methodical. And his father was a mean bastard, mechanically, thoughtlessly mean. A zombie, grey-skinned and puffy, his face like a collapsed mask. A man who'd swallowed his own death. And they had the nerve to act as if *he* was weird!

When they went into their bedroom at night—it didn't bear thinking about . . . Mum unzipping her mum-suit, and Dad slipping into his grave . . .

If only, he thought—and it was not the sort of thing he'd tell anyone, not the sort of chat he'd swap with, say, Nick—if only *they* were my parents.

He hung about the espresso machine, hoping to catch a glimpse of them—Nick giving him the odd playful flick with his towel, showing off his moves—until Bob came over.

'How many times? Eh? How many times?'

'I was thinking,' Ben lied. 'We need a dishwasher, for the kitchen. You know, a machine.'

It was easy to get Bob going, to distract him.

'Dishwashingmachines! The noise, the waste! I've been forced to capitulate with the bar. But so eco-nasty!'

The sick old fuck, Ben thought, smiling to himself as he went back out to his steamy galley, and plunged his hands into the water. The sick old fuck. You couldn't reason with him.

Nick stuck his head round the corner, and leered. 'Nice one, Stonewash. You're a shifty dude.'

'Yeah, right, Nick,' he said. That was the level of conversation. That was it.

One day he was going to get out of there, Ben told himself. Out of the wet, swampy kitchen, out of Bob's menagerie. Out of everywhere he knew, clear away. Where? Somewhere else.

He came home from work, and stood at the doorway and watched his parents gaping at the TV: Dad dozing, dreaming his sour dreams, Mum doing a refresher course. That's not how *they* would do it, he told himself. That's not the sort of lousy life they'd live.

He thought about them all the time now. How they glowed. On the bus, heading into work, in the narrow kitchen, washing dish after steaming dish, at breakfast, avoiding his father's eyes. He thought about them while he endured his mother's cooking; her droning dinner voice, so that the TV's shout was a relief. That's not what *she'd* cook, he'd tell himself. That's not what *they* would eat. He was full of them; but only his fantasy of them after all.

Then, like a dream he had, the blonde man came for him. He stood at the bar and smiled. He tipped his head to one side, his face soft and careless, and said, 'We'd like you to come to supper tonight.'

'I—' said Ben.

'When you're through,' said the man, smiling and smiling, and indicated the door. He left then, his cream-coloured jacket slung casually over his shoulder.

All the way out to the north shore, in the leather-smelling car, past glinting lit gardens and tree-shaded houses, the boy and the man sat silent, listening to their own thoughts.

I am going home, Ben told himself. Home.

How did they recognise me?

You'll find that out later, he told himself.

His heart pounded, lightly, a joyous rapping at his chest. Here I am! Here I am! it said.

He sniffed his fingers delicately. They stank. He lay them beneath his jeans, in between the steady weight of his thighs and the softness of the new seat.

Deep into the night they drove, the car smoothly hugging the curves of the highway, and down a deep dark hill. House lights winked from time to time, and then, abruptly, they pulled into a semi-circular drive, in front of a two-storey white doll's house. A warm circle of light spilled from the porch. Ben imagined the tan labrador leaping to greet them.

There was music coming from the house, something old and romantic, with an orchestra playing. They got out, and closed their doors simultaneously, and the man smiled at him, as if he knew how he was feeling. They went in, through a pale wooden door, over plush pale pile, and into a room with bone-coloured couches.

He stared around the room, astounded at the lack of knick-knacks. The dog, he told himself, must be asleep.

Outside, in its kennel. And *she* must be in the kitchen, preparing the supper. Which would be very light, he told himself, and not slimy. But when he saw her, naked, except for a tightly laced red leather bustier, splayed out on a couch, he did not know what to tell himself.

JESSICA LANGE IN 'FRANCES'

Christos Tsiolkas

There's not much happening outside the window. There is just sound and violence. I'm looking down on cars slowly making their way up the street, stalled by the trams. People are shopping. It's a mid-afternoon, mid-week crowd. The sun is still high in the sky; a thick sheet of heat.

The cat is asleep, sprawled across my lap. I'm touching my lips on the cool glass of my water, sniffing the drops of lemon. A drunk girl is cursing the world, stomping through the crowd below. She's fat, the Adidas shirt can't hide the flab. I'm stroking the cat, drinking the water.

I can see Dirty Harry; he's knocking into people, drunk, they're cursing him. He's eating paper. He eats it in strips, tearing it apart. He sucks on it, chews it, swallows it all up.

'Why do you eat it?' I asked him once. Drunk.

'I like it.' He asked me for another drink. 'It lines my stomach,' he chuckled, 'slows down the effect of the booze.' He was scratching at a soaked beer coaster, scraping off the cardboard and rolling the scraps along his tongue. Washed it down with a whiskey.

The telephone rings and I push the cat off my lap. She falls quick, licks a paw and wags her bum at me. Offended. I grab the receiver.

'It's me.'

I'm silent.

'Aren't you talking to me?'

'Maybe.' I give in, I can feel a smile breaking through. He senses it, the bastard can always sense it.

'You glad I called?'

'Where were you?' I'm not giving in, not straight away.

'Got pissed.'

'I figured that.'

'Oh, don't start with that shit.'

My smile is gone.

'I waited up.'

'I said I'm sorry.'

'No, you didn't.'

'I just did.'

The cat has jumped on the coffee table and nudged herself into the fruit bowl. I'm lighting a cigarette, silent.

'You're smoking?'

I breathe out.

'It sure sounds sexy.' Low, very very low voice. Late-night movie and a joint voice. I giggle. Forgiving him.

The party was loud, crashing percussion on the stereo. It

was liquid alcohol in every room, the atmosphere, thick and wet. Drunk people dancing, drunk people shouting, drunk people slumped over armchairs and couches. I turned up late, after a midnight session at the pictures. Sober. I weaved through the couples in the narrow hall-way, made my way to the bathroom and tried to find a beer, but I was out of luck. Only empty cans and cigarette butts in the icy bathtub slush.

'Looking for piss?'

He held out his stubbie for me. I hesitated.

'G'on,' he urged me, 'take a swig.'

I took some. He walked over, clumsily, to the toilet bowl and unzipped. I took another sip and watched him. His jeans were too big, baggy, so I couldn't make out the shape of his arse but his black T-shirt stretched tight around his hefty shoulders. He is a strong man. He took a long piss and he turned around to look at me. He winked and held out his hand. I walked over and handed him the stubbie and, still pissing, he took a swig before handing it back. We smiled, together.

'Finish it,' he said. The stream of urine slowed down to a trickle. He shook out the last drops and left without washing his hands. I noticed that. I can't piss without washing up afterwards. A habit of a lifetime.

I found Leah in one of the bedrooms, sharing a joint with some of her friends from college. I sat down next to her, put my hand across her waist and kissed her neck.

'How was the movie?'

'Good,' I answered, 'fun.'

'What did you see?' one of her friends asked me. I can't remember her name. Sheila, or Shandra? Maybe just Sandra.

I told her.

The man in the bathroom was now standing in the

doorway, stroking the face of a very beautiful neo-hippie girl. She had glitter on her cheeks and he was tracing the stardust. I looked away, pretending to ignore him.

He was pretending to ignore me.

A grape has fallen into the cat's drink bowl. Black hairs are swimming around in it. I pour out a dish of dry food for her and wash the bowl in the sink. The grape falls into the plughole and I squash it down with my thumb, watch it drop through the grill. Some nights, especially when it's rained, slugs swarm around her bowl, getting into the meat, drowning in her water. I pick them up with toilet paper. I hate touching them, hate the stiff, sticky residue they leave on my fingers. He doesn't mind at all, picks them up and chucks them straight back into the garden, wipes his fingers across his jeans. Leaving silver streaks.

The cat sniffs at the dry biscuits, eats a few, then leaves the dish alone. I close the laundry door, walk through the garden and go out the back gate. The kitchen-hand from the Vietnamese restaurant next door is sitting on a milk crate, smoking a cigarette.

'How you going?' I ask him.

'Alright.' He drops his voice and points to the terrace behind us. 'But I wish I wasn't working in this shit-hole.' A strong wind is blowing stale hot air hard onto my face. I smell the oil and spices from the kitchen, they're sinking all around me.

It takes forty minutes to walk to his place. I arrive hot, sweating and in a bad temper. He is out in the back garden, a wet cloth wrapped around his head, empty beer cans around his feet. He's wearing his underpants, nothing else. His white underpants, his very brown skin. He looks up at me, squints, grinning.

'How are ya?' He doesn't wait for a reply. 'Feel like going to the pub, mate? I'm all out of piss.'

They had put chairs and a few cushions out in the backyard. Scented candles were melting wax over a small coffee table. I left Leah, her friends, their boring conversation about school and exams and gossip. I was stoned. There was no-one else in the yard, the party had thinned out and I was enjoying the solitude. It wasn't much of a garden, a few patches of herbs. I lay down on a cushion, looking at the stars. A half-moon.

'Had enough, eh, mate?'

He sat down next to me. I didn't bother to get up. He passed me his joint. We sat in silence for minutes, listening to the music, a tranced reggae. We smoked the joint and I sat up. His eyes, black eyes, not brown, not olive, but black, were shining bright, mirroring the candlelight. There was stubble on his baby face. It suited him. He was looking straight at me, hard.

'Enjoying the party?' An inane question, but I wanted to break through the tension. This silence was getting uncomfortable.

'Where you from?'

I didn't expect that question. He kept on looking into me.

'Melbourne.'

'No, I mean where your parents from?'

And you, where are you from? That's what I was wondering.

'Jordan,' I answered, 'my father's from Jordan and my mother was born in Egypt.'

He whistled. 'Jordanian-Egyptian. Very sexy.'

I laughed. 'I'm a mongrel. Mum's half-French and half-Greek. I'm a genetic soup.'

65

'That's why you're so good-looking.' He said it softly. But every word was clear, direct.

I got scared. But I liked him calling me good-looking.

'Are you going to come home with me?'

I wanted a cigarette. I started fumbling through my pockets. My pack was squashed. He offered me one of his. I took one, slowly, careful not to touch his hand.

'Are you going to come home with me?' Again, soft. Same steady insistence. I pointed towards the house, to the party.

'That's my girlfriend in there.'

That's when he looked away, pulled his knees up to his chest and sunk his head. He said something, said it to some place down deep inside himself.

'I can't hear you.' I wanted him to look up, not be sad. I wanted him to look at me again.

He lifted his face. A wicked large grin.

'You still haven't answered my fucking question.'

'Fuck you!' I scream it, stressing both words with exclamation marks. I'm pacing up and down his concrete shit-hole of a backyard.

'I'm out of money, all right! All I did was fucking ask you to shout me some cans. You don't want to do it, fine. Leave it then.'

'It's the way you ask me. No hellos, no how are you, no nothing. I'm sick of it.'

'You want a kiss, baby?' Sarcastic tone, spat out in a faggot voice.

'Ah, you're a prick.'

A grunt.

'You're a prick!' I'm screaming it out.

'Enough.' I can tell he's angry now, real angry. I

shouldn't push it. But it's hot, too hot, I'm tired and yeah, fuck the arsehole I could do with a kiss, some affection.

'You're nothing but a drunk.'

He stands up, abrupt. Automatic, his hand becomes a fist. I jump back. And he laughs.

'Come on, come on.' He leans over, kisses my lips. I lick his, we touch tongues and he pulls away.

'I'll cook you dinner.'

'You serious?' I'm dubious.

'Oath.' He crosses himself.

I go down the road, get him his beer.

I told Leah I was tired, a little sick. She was having a good time, going off dancing, and after a few moments of stroking my face, holding my hand, we kissed good-bye. She asked no questions about him; she thought nothing of him walking out with me.

We walked through parkland. There were possums everywhere and he stopped in front of one, crouched, and whispered quietly to it. It looked at him, transfixed, but he stumbled, fell, and the possum ran fast up a tree. I put a hand on his shoulder, to steady him, and he took it and helped himself up. He didn't let go.

I looked around, nervous, felt spied upon. His hand felt rough, enormous, so different to Leah's light touch. I took my hand away.

He took it back and I stopped being frightened. I noticed the thick hair on his arm and I traced my fingers through it. The heaviness of his body. We kept walking, his arm around my shoulder, staggering, mostly silent all the way to his house. Except he asked me what football team I barracked for.

'Essendon.'

He nodded.

'And you?'

'Carlton.'

And that was it, we kept walking, through the park, down back alleys, all the way to his house. He was humming songs I recognised.

He put his finger to his lips and navigated me quietly to his bedroom. The light, when he switched it on, was far too bright. A naked globe hung low from the ceiling. He sat on the unmade mattress. I remained standing, uncomfortable, looking around the bedroom walls. A few snapshots, a poster of *Taxi Driver* and old record sleeves of Lou Reed, Hunters and Collectors. *Human Frailty*. I looked everywhere but at him. Until he started stripping.

His body was firm but not tight. He took off his T-shirt and I looked at his chest, almost hairless, the nipples lightly hanging. The three small folds of his belly. I felt a locker-room shyness; caught stealing illicit glances.

I looked away to a torn-out picture from a magazine, on the wall opposite me. The edges were ragged. Jessica Lange, her gaze intense, straight into the camera. He was unzipping my trousers, kissing my cock through my briefs. My cock remained limp and I was blushing.

'Good movie,' I said, making conversation. He stopped kissing.

He looked over his shoulder and up at the picture. 'Yeah, ace movie. A fucking classic. What they did to her, you know. Frances Farmer, that's the worse thing you can do to someone, to take away their soul.'

I was looking down at him. His hair was limp. Tenderness, I was feeling tenderness; the footballer's shoulders and inside them the little boy. I stroked his hair, his face, and

we were kissing and

his mouth was harsh, not a girl's mouth, and his body was hard as it pressed against

me, covering me, but the skin was tender, like touching the underneath of bark

and I thought a few times, as we were making love, that

fuck, it's a man, this is a man

but our bodies worked together, and he kept kissing my eyelids and his cock tasted

warm in my mouth, and I liked him coming all over me, groaning and swearing loudly,

repeating

oh man oh man oh man

and as I was coming I had my eyes closed but I was digging my mouth into his neck and

I had to stop myself screaming, so I bit into him, because what I wanted to scream was

something about love. Which is terror, which made me want to hit him, kick him. And then I came, the feelings stopped and I slumped to numb.

He got up, switched off the light, grabbed his T-shirt and wiped the come off me. I lay there, still. There was a car outside his window jackhammering an ignition.

He held me, his arm wrapped around my chest. I was smelling his sweat.

'Are you going to tell your girlfriend?'

I said no. The metallic night light was making ghosts of the pictures on his wall.

'Is this the first time you've slept with a guy, mate?'

I nodded.

'Me too. I mean I've had sex with guys before. But you're the first guy I've brought home.'

I was aware of the pressure of his thigh on mine, coarse hair digging into my skin.

'You believe me, don't ya?'

'It doesn't matter.' I remember thinking, women taste of nectar, men smell like citrus.

'Of course it fucking matters.' He whispered it. 'Of course it matters.'

I fell asleep, in his arms, watching Jessica's hair dance silver.

It's ten o'clock, night has definitely fallen and my stomach is rumbling. He's back from another trip to the pub. There's a cop show from England on the television but I'm not taking it in. He's lying on the couch drinking. I notice his belly's getting bigger.

'You're getting fat.'

He pats his stomach and lets out a Tarzan yodel.

'I'm hungry.'

'Order some pizza.'

'I'm tired of pizza, you said you'd cook.'

'Can't be bothered. Order a pizza.'

'Who's going to pay?' Fucking user. I don't say that. I don't want to believe it.

I get up off the floor and walk into the kitchen. There's dry bread in the cupboard. Two tomatoes, a lettuce, a jar of mustard and some tinnies in the fridge. That's it. I walk back into the loungeroom and position myself in front of the TV screen.

'Let's go out. Get a bite to eat.'

'Get out of the fucking way.'

I stand there.

'What the fuck is up with you?'

'I'm hungry.'

'Well go out and get something to eat.' He opens another can of beer.

'Come with me.'

'Look, mate, I just want to watch some teev. I'm not in a mood to go out.'

'You were last night.' Without me. I've not forgiven him.

'Last night was different. Now get out of the way and let me watch the show.'

I don't move.

'You're a drunk.'

He takes a long sip, he's silent, watching me.

'You're also a pig.'

He finishes the can in two long gulps, throwing the liquid down his throat.

'You smell, always stink of piss.'

'That's enough.'

I sense the outrage in his voice. I don't move. I keep going.

'And you're dumb. Dumb as dogshit.'

'I said, enough!'

I keep taunting him. Call him more names, throw up my anger, call him poofter, call him faggot, I keep yelling until he bolts up

and all this happens so quick that I don't have time to run not even time to plead though I hear myself scream-ing something before he's hurtling into me and I'm kicking but he's stronger and bigger and tougher and knows how to fight and he cracks me sharp across my face and as I fall his knee crashes into my stomach and that's it, I'm crying, flat on my arse and it's not even that it hurts very much until he punches me in the middle of my mouth so my teeth bite on my tongue, I'm tasting blood, and he turns me over and twists my arm around my back and with his free hand he tears at my hair banging my head on the carpet till he hears something break and he lets go, I slump on the floor.

Then he slips my shorts around my knees and slides his fingers up my arse, so hard, it's like a punch going right up me, in me, through me, and he tries to slide his cock in and I'm struggling, squirming, screaming so he bangs my head down on the carpet again and again until I've shut up.

The first five thrusts,

I'm counting them because they're slicing through my gut,

it feels like a blade has torn through my bowels and up to my stomach but all I do is squeal high like a pig and then the thrusts become a pounding

and I prefer the hammer to the blade because the pain is duller and I'm waiting for it to finish, the television is on, and a cop is running after some black kid who's been dealing drugs on a housing estate, out of nowhere I'm hearing a shit Bryan Adams song in my head, and as the thrusts become more rapid he is throwing himself deeper into me and all I'm thinking is please god, don't let me shit, oh please god please don't let me shit please god don't let me shit.

He comes, goes soft inside me, and falls inert on top of me. There is a wetness on the back of my neck, maybe his tears, but maybe, probably, just spit.

The cop get the black kid.

Neither of us is making a sound. I'd be sick if he tried to talk to me. There's not a word. All I'm aware of is the acrid stink of the alcohol. There's blood in my mouth, I spit it out.

I watch the television, watch the red dial on the video recorder clock down the time to midnight. He's falling asleep. I won't move till I'm sure it's deep sleep. I'm counting down the red digits. I hear the stifled snores shudder on my neck. Slowly, carefully, I shift from under him and though he stirs, he rolls over and is back to sleep. I'm dripping blood all over the carpet, over him.

I get up and wash my face in the bathroom sink. In the mirror I am bloated. I move quickly through the house, taking the alarm clock I lent him, taking the book I'm reading, taking my shirts, my socks, my underwear. I'm erasing myself from this house.

I pause at the three strips of photos pinned to the bedroom mirror. Black and whites from a photo booth. I take one strip, shove everything into a plastic bag and leave the bedroom. But I return, to take the picture of Jessica Lange. I'm making it mine.

The television is playing the news. Trade conference in Asia. He's still asleep, heavy drunk snoring. I lean over him, and his black hair is sweat-plastered to his forehead. I can still see it, still fucking see it: his face is sweet. I lean over closer, trying to get through and back to him. I try to smell him but I can only make out the alcohol, the mouldy yeast of beer. I am, finally, repelled.

The first taxi-driver takes one look at me and speeds off. The second takes me, but refuses to talk to me. I don't mind. I sit in the back, hugging myself tight to stop the shivering.

The cat is meowing for food. I feed her fish and notice the slugs. One monster in particular. Its thick elastic body has climbed over the rim and sits inside the bowl, oozing filth. I grab a tissue from the toilet, pick it up, holding it far away from me. The cat ignores me, she's lapping up her food. I take the slug, wrapped in tissue, into the loo and throw it in the toilet bowl. I piss and I make sure I aim my stream directly for the slug, torch it with my urine. When I'm finished I flush, watch the water, the tissue, the slug spin round, round, round. Then all of it, abruptly, is gone.

The room is hot upstairs and I open the window. The fierceness from the street comes rushing in; dance music from across the road, the squeals and horns of cars. Another crazy man is yelling out obscenities. Teenagers are laughing. My mouth is hurting, swelling. My gut, my arse, they are fire.

I toss the plastic bag at the back of the wardrobe, then drown it under jumpers and blankets. But I make sure to retrieve the picture of Jessica Lange. I run my thumb on its shredded edges. I clumsily light a cigarette and put the smouldering tip through the picture. I watch the hole expand, burning her mouth, her chin, her angry eyes. As the picture becomes flame I throw it in an ashtray, mash it up, turn it to ash, to dust.

I sit and watch the traffic flow. The night is warm but a breeze is blowing in from the south, off the ocean. I lean out the window. I'm still fire. I pack ice into a glass, fill it up with water. Again. It's no good. Nothing helps to cool me down.

ANOTHER SATISFIED CUSTOMER

THE DESERTERS

Clare Mendes

I check me watch and see it's around midday. I crack open a beer.

Normally I'd say, midday, that's too early for a drink, but it's a scorcher and business is slow. It's a scorcher, and I say that's different to a corker because in a scorcher people get this idea into their heads that it's too hot to even pull over to the side of the road, they wanna keep on driving, driving; but in a corker everyone drinks, man, woman and dog. They'll be driving past and they see me and ya can just hear all the misses saying, with their windows wound down and their bare legs stuck up on the dashboard for air, ya can just hear them saying, 'Pull over will ya Fred? I thought I spotted a bar back there, I wanna drink—pull over will ya?' And they do pull over, and sometimes both husband and wife are so desperate for a beer they'll swing their bare feet out the sides of the car and hop up to me Desert Bar without feeling a stone or a burr underfoot. That's how much they'll want a beer.

Ya get those ones who just happen to be driving down Deadwood Road and then ya get ya other ones. Carloads full of people, and there's never any pattern cos ya can get a Volvo then ya get a campervan and then it'll be another Volvo, and all these ones, what they're doing is coming in off the highway. They're thirsty; they look up and they see the sign I painted meself and put out there, and they're thinking, *Now that's just what I need after all this travelling, a nice cold beer*. The sign's good like that cos underneath the words 'Just opened! Doug's Desert Bar' I've painted a jug of beer with the biggest head ya ever dreamed about.

Like I said, patterns are hard to gauge at this present point in time. Trends and that. When you've only been open six months ya can't expect to have ya finger on the pulse. When the Standard opened in Broken Hill forty odd years ago I was there, and we didn't need no fancy sign to let everyone know we were in business, we just gave out free pints to any bloke who looked dry. I couldn't afford free beer on me opening day here. Maybe that's why nobody came along.

But word's catching on. I reckon any day now folks are gonna hear about Doug's Desert Bar even before they leave Broken Hill. Before they leave Sydney. When business picks up a bit, I'll be able to afford to do a bit of self-promotion and first thing I'm gonna do is get some photos taken of meself standing under me sign and I'll send them to the Tourist Bureau and say, 'Print this, will ya? Cos one day Doug's Desert Bar'll be on the map.'

Ya can get anything put on the map. Evie's brother

Jack, his general store got put on two maps and he didn't even have a blinking sign.

Word'll catch on.

But even while business is a bit slow I wouldn't say it's not rewarding. The best part of working at the Standard was getting to meet people from all walks of life and nothing changes, cos even being a one-man show and stationed out in the desert like I am, I get a good mix of trade.

They're all on their way to White Cliffs. Opals are there, and where there's opals there's money and where there's money there's tourists. Maybe I should've gone into opals. But some of them's just going cos White Cliffs is a place to go, and cos they've got underground houses there. 'What does *my* joint look like?' I said to this Volvo driver a couple of weeks back. 'A circus tent?' But he says he doesn't wanna see inside *my* underground. I know I've mentioned this Volvo bloke before but as with any job, some customers stick in ya head. Maybe it was last month he came.

But for a businessman, he had one hot head on his shoulders. 'What's this road called?' he asks me.

'Deadwood Road,' I tell him.

He looks up. He looks down. 'I don't know how I could've done that,' he says. 'I don't know why I didn't just stay on the highway.' He looks up and down me road again, then he says, 'This is a strange place to put a bar. I doubt it'll take off.'

Another sceptic. Ya learn to cope; I do it by taking his photo. He frowns at me Polaroid. 'What do you plan on doing with that photo?'

His missis is in the passenger seat, flapping herself with a magazine. 'We've got to be in White Cliffs by five, Dennis,' she says. 'I don't want to be driving when the kangaroos come out.'

But the bloke bought three beers. And they went to his head, I reckon maybe he saw pink kangaroos after that.

That was a corker day, that one. I got three customers. Like I've said, ya corker days are the best. Almost all of the cars that go past stop and buys a drink. I sell orange juice too, for the kiddies, and if they buy two glasses I give them a strap of licorice and when people see that, especially the mothers, they decide I'm not some eccentric recluse who decided to set up a bar at the side of the road one day. They look round the bar and they see me certificate of registration up on the counter and they see the tarp I've stretched out over the whole works and the nifty UV-protection shadecloth that closes it in on all but the fourth side. They see I'm responsible, and serious about me business.

I paid through the eye teeth for that UV set-up. At the hardware joint in Broken Hill, me mate Jim Bailey, he'd never heard of the stuff and I said to him, 'Well they reckon if I wanna proper bar license, if I'm gonna be legitimate, I have to buy it, Jim.' So he orders it in. And it actually works in more ways than one, cos when the folks stop off for their beer and they see the 'UV-protective measures in place'—that's what the Department calls them—they're more inclined to hang round the bar for a bit before getting into their cars and driving off. And that means instead of just serving up beers, I get to chat.

Mostly people just wanna chat about themselves. They tell ya where they've come from and where they're going and they give ya times and dates of arrival, names of hotels and caravan parks they're gonna stay in—heck, they even tell ya where they're gonna fill up on petrol and how many ks they get to the gallon. But I've been a barman for more years than I can remember, and I've worked out that when folks tell ya stuff like that, what they're doing is setting their minds at rest. And when I was working at the Standard the one thing I learnt was, as a barman ya paid to serve and listen.

So I listen. And every so often when they finish rattling off their ruddy itineraries and they look down the Deadwood Road, to that point on the horizon where the sun sinks down orange like it's bending to kiss the beautiful, burnt, flat land, I say to them, 'Can ya honestly think of a better place to set up a bar? Right in the middle of the desert?'

I keep me fingers crossed. I always hope they'll say, 'What a ripper idea Doug!' or 'Who would've thought of it?'

But what they usually say is: 'This is a strange place to put a bar. I don't reckon it'll take off.'

I take their photo. Revenge is sweet.

They tell me their travel plans, these people, but none of them asks me where I'm going or what my dreams are. None of them cares who Doug Attiwell is. They just care that when they're thirsty, Doug can serve up a cold one. And some days when business is quiet like today, I turn on me stool and take a sip on me beer and I look at me underground house, hiding there in the sun with the carport sticking up wonky to the left hand side of it. I look at the pile of rubble that marks where the steps go down and at the little garden out front that Evie put in before she passed on—the flowers are still growing, they just seem to be growing out dead—and I think to meself, *So what's so special about me life to make a customer ask questions?*

But I ask them questions. Doesn't matter if he's the most boring so-and-so this side of the Black Stump, like them tourists who go sailing down the road in their brand new Volvos, thinking they're gonna make their fortune in opals at White Cliffs. Doesn't matter, cos I've always been of the opinion that a day without conversation is a day in hell. Everyone's a stranger till ya make them ya friend. And living out here, where there's not another neighbour for a hundred kilometres either direction, nothing but beautiful burnt, flat land as far as the eye can see, ya can't afford to treat no-one like a stranger.

Jim from the hardware store, he says to me whenever I go into Broken Hill, he says, 'Don't ya regret moving out there Doug? Must get damn lonely. Why don't ya come back here now Evie's gone? Reckon they'd give ya a shift at ya old pub.' But I say to him, 'Don't ya remember what they said to me Jim, the blokes at the Standard? "It's a strange place to put a bar, Doug. Don't reckon it'll take off." That's what they said when I bought me land and built me underground. "It's a fool idea, bloke of your age to start up a business that risky. Beside, don't ya know they're building a highway that's gonna bypass Deadwood Road? Folks'll take the highway to White Cliffs, Doug. You won't get no customers," they said.

'But ya gotta go with ya gut feeling don't ya? And I'd always said to them, all the years I was working at the Standard, "I've got this gut feeling that a bar out in the middle of the desert'd take off like nobody's business. Land's dirt cheap to buy, ya got ya bustling passing trade, and God knows ya got ya thirsty clients—what can go wrong?" And in the end they were wrong, weren't they Jim?'

'Yeah,' he agrees. He can't believe it himself, how

me business has taken off. Though of course I exaggerate me success a bit, ya gotta tell a few red herrings if ya want people to respect ya. I wonder sometimes if Jim's a bit jealous, stuck in this store while I'm out in the fresh air. He scratches his head. 'But don't ya get lonely out there Doug?'

'Na,' I tell him. 'I've got me five minute mates, haven't I?'

It's one o'clock and I've just served a five minute mate.

Family in a four-wheel drive. Drove by, stopped a little way up the road. Bloke sends the missis trotting back up the road, and I get out me best glass and put the nice new bottle of lemonade up on the counter and put on me best smile as well, cos it's been quiet as buggery today and I could do with a bit of a natter.

She only wants directions though. 'Is this the way to Menindee?' she says.

'Heck no,' I say. 'Ya miles off.' She's a pretty enough thing, with a face that's pink with sunburn. There's a big welt across her shoulder from where the seat belt's been cutting into it. 'See that road?' I point over her shoulder, past the dried-up creek bed where Evie used to sit each evening on her cushion and sketch the sunset. 'Ya take that road south, love. Youse've got a three-hour drive ahead.'

'Oh,' she says. 'Thank you.'

Then, just as I'm about to say, How about a shandy on the house? she looks round me bar and she looks up and down and round again and she says, 'Isn't this a strange place to set up a bar? I can't see it taking off.'

I pull out me Polaroid. 'Say cheese,' I say to me five minute friend. I snap her photo. She glares at me.

Five minute friends. They can sting ya like lifelong

ones can. As she goes back to her car, I feel like yelling out to her, 'What do ya reckon, should I open up shop in Antarctica? Or Greenland maybe, ya reckon I'd get a few thirsty Eskimos beating down me doors for a cold one?' But I keep me thoughts to meself cos that's part of being a good barman, ya listen and don't answer back. And like I always say, a day without conversation is a day in hell.

Ya should be counting ya lucky stars she took a wrong turn, I say to meself. Be grateful for small mercies, that's what Evie used to say.

But when I think of what the woman said to me, I open up another beer and gulp it right down, and I don't care if it's only five past one and it doesn't look good for a barman to be drinking on the job because by God nothing gets me down as much as members of the public who don't believe in me.

Cos I'm on a goldmine here. And I know any day now, business is gonna boom.

I reckon it's the tall poppy syndrome. People in this country like seeing an honest man make good, but as soon as he gets too successful—*chop!* Like that bloke in the Volvo. He gave me his two bits worth. But some of the best businesses have been built in the face of adversity, and I've come up with a way of turning me customers' pessimism into something positive.

That's what me photos are for. Every time one of them finishes up their beer and says to me over the rim, 'This is a strange place to stick a bar. I don't reckon it's gonna take off,' I swallow me anger and say, 'Hold it a minny. Now, say ch-e-e-e-se,' and I pull out me Polaroid from underneath the counter and take a snap.

Course they don't smile too often. Most of the time they just blink; had one bloke one time, I think he was the bloke in the Volvo, who went all funny when I took his photo and wanted to know what I was gonna use it for. But this was Evie's camera, and I'm never giving it up. She used to say, 'The Lord gave us cameras so we can hold on to the past,' and that's what I'm doing with these mug shots stuck up on this piece of chipboard behind the bar. They're little pieces of the past. Or at least they will be a couple of years down the track, when the Desert Bar strikes gold; and it doesn't matter that half these folks've got their eyes closed or snarls on their faces, cos that's what pessimism looks like, doesn't it? The day this bar becomes famous and all the TV reporters are out here, I'll hold up me photo board to the cameras and I'll say to the viewing population, 'Success is the best revenge.'

Cos one day, the joke'll be on them.

It's three o'clock. I dunno where two o'clock went; it just up and disappeared. Went flying down the road with the flock of cockies that comes swooping past me every afternoon, laughing at me. I'd take a photo of them but that'd look pretty stupid, when this bar comes good, to say as I hold up each photo, 'Success is the best revenge. There was this bloke, and this sheila—oh yeah, and this pack of cockies who was always singing out ridicules to me.' So today as usual I let the birds fly past without turning them into instant celebrities, but I reckon I must've been holding on to the Polaroid for a good hour cos when I wake up me hands are stiff.

It's warm beer makes ya doze off like that. I give meself a mental hiding for the third time that day, cos a barman shouldn't drink on the job, but ten minutes pass, fifteen; at 3.30 I'm still holding the camera.

And wondering.

A lizard comes slinking along in the grass. There's lots of lizards out at the moment and if this was a bar for lizards I'd be making a killing cos even when it's a scorcher they head for the shade of the bar in scores and no matter how many flies are buzzing round their heads all they've got the energy for is to poke out their skinny blue tongues and lap up the beer as it comes off the counter. But they're the worst kinds of customers cos not only don't they pay, they also don't say nothing.

And like I've always said, a day without conversation is a day in hell.

This one who's visiting me now, I've called him Jim. He looks like he's been hanging under the eaves of a hardware store—got a splash of red on his belly that could be from earth, but it could be paint that's done it too. I grab hold of his back leg now and say, 'How are ya Jim ya old bastard? When ya gonna visit me like ya said ya would?' cos it's going on a year now he's been saying he'll drop out here for a visit and no sign of him. Not a trace.

There's no trace of anyone on the horizon. More cars are going down the highway this week than last week. I think about making me sign bigger. I think about getting new tumblers and serving up nuts and them pretzel things.

At four o'clock I'm still holding on to the camera. I hang it from its big leather strap round me neck. I pack up the bar. I lift the trestle table off the two big drums and I take down the tarp and I roll up the UV shadecloth, tighter than usual. Bar's packed up. I put the bottles of beer back in the wheelbarrow.

A gust of wind blows dirt into me eyes and this blowie flies into me mouth and buzzes a kind of conversation with me teeth before I crunch it hard. Spit it out.

THE DESERTERS

As I walk to the underground with me bar dragging behind me, there's red soil flicking up from me heels where normally it sits quiet. And the Polaroid's banging against me chest.

Today's the day I take a photo of her.

Her name's Ruby. She's not old, maybe eighteen. She's sitting cool as a cucumber up against the wall of the living room; I walk in and show her me hands, black under the nails. I take off me hat and show her the way me hair's sticking to me head with all the heat and the hours sitting under the sun and I say to her, 'You'd look like this too after a decent day's work.' She doesn't hear me. She's doped up on one of them drugs the kids take. She's got the music on, some rowdy station, and she's staring at the calendar on the wall like she's willing some fairy to come along and flick over the page from February to March. But the picture of the waterfall stays put. It's a good calendar. Each page's got something cool and refreshing on it—I got it free with me shadecloth.

'Hey,' I say to her. I give her a nudge; she doesn't move. 'March's got a nice juicy watermelon on it. But you won't be here that long.'

'Nnng,' she says.

Already she's been here three days. Arrived late Friday with the truckie going to White Cliffs, now that's four days—four days and I still haven't taken her photo. But I keep hoping she's gonna scrub up a bit better than she does, when each day she just looks worse. Like a snake shedding its skin. One day it was off with the leather sandals, next it was the satin shirt. Third day she didn't bother sticking on her nice red lipstick—now that lipstick, it was the only thing added colour to her face and I say to her, 'I thought ya name was Ruby?' and she nods, real slow. She shows me a knuckle loaded with red garnet rings.

Dunno what else she can take off. Maybe her hair, cos even that looks like it'd come out with ten good hard yanks. That's how many she's got, ten strands. They're stuck together with glue or something, and on half of them there's these plastic beads—Evie'd turn over in her grave if she could see what this girl's done to herself.

I don't even reckon she's seen soap today. I've only got two shots left. She'll be a waste of film.

She was only meant to stay a night but it's been four days. I didn't want her to stay here at all, once I found out the sort of sheila she was. She was a talker, that's what got me in. 'Hasn't stopped since Silverton,' the truckie said to me. He was a decent bloke himself, by which I mean he was a decent drinker. He'd put away three pots even before I'd seen the girl sitting in the passenger side of the semi. And he didn't think a desert bar was a bad idea. He reckons he was dying of thirst: I saved him. *Saved* him.

When he says that, I give him a beer on the house plus a packet of chips same as I give the kiddies. I don't ask him why he's driving down Deadwood Road instead of the highway.

And this isn't a five minute mate, cos we're talking a good half hour. It's the best natter I've had since I bought the last lot of beer in the Hill. But I'm no fool, I know that's like paying for conversation. This bloke though, he wants to talk to me. He says what a great idea a desert bar is. Then he says he'd like to set up his own. Then he says, 'I can drop her here with you, can't I?'

I think for a sec he's talking about his blue singlet, cos he's taken it off and he's flapping it over his head, round his shoulders, everywhere the flies are landing. But then he points towards the girl.

He said she was a talker.

She was slumped against the window, asleep. 'She's worn herself out I reckon, Doug,' he says to me. 'All her gasbagging. Opals are what she's into. Opals and gems and precious stones, Doug.' He kept using me name. 'Says she's a fortune teller and she's on her way to White Cliffs. Says she's stocking up on supplies—they use stuff like that in their fortune telling, Doug. Now I'm a quiet bloke meself, Doug, I don't reckon I can put up with a sheila who wants to talk and talk.'

Seems she'd worn herself out to the point where she needed help getting down from the truck. And then the truck's cleared off and she's standing there with this long black dress of hers blowing in the wind.

She says just two things. The first is: 'Where am I?'

'Deadwood Road,' I tell her. 'Ya can stay here till another truckie comes by. That one liked his peace and quiet.'

She looks down the road to where the cloud of dust is settling. Her pupils are ringed red like the dust. She looks over at me bar and that's when she says the second thing. 'This is a dumb place to put a bar. I don't reckon it'll take off.'

She passes out on the ground.

And that was Friday arvo. Today's Tuesday. She hasn't spoken a word in between. All the time she's doped out.

I wanna take a photo of Ruby for what she said, but I can't get her to keep her head up.

Ruby spends all day looking spaced out.

When I come in of an afternoon, she's usually got

out her crystals. She just stares at them. She keeps them in a little velvet bag that she hangs from her wrist. She doesn't hardly notice me.

It's only when I put the pot on to boil that she comes to life. She comes to life whenever she hears anything bubbling. Maybe she's a witch, not a fortune teller. Maybe she's one of them new white witches and when she's not here, freeloading off me, she's sitting in front of a cauldron boiling up people's fingers. The idea puts a chill through me, but then ya don't know who ya letting under ya roof do ya?

It's been six days now. Or maybe it's seven, maybe eight. One thing's for sure, next semi that comes through, Ruby's on it. If she's tough enough to hitch all the way from Silverton she shouldn't have no problems getting to White Cliffs. I cut up yesterday's roo and toss it in; it smells funny, but I haven't had any tucker all day and she's too dopey to notice. At the *ker-plonk!* up comes her head and I think for a minny she's gonna say a couple words but she just says, 'Nnng,' and starts twisting each of them rings of hers.

It's a sign of life I suppose. I stir me roo. 'You'll get some nice-looking stones in White Cliffs,' I say to her. 'Opals. Gems. Boil up some silver and ya can make ya own rings. You'd have access to a big pot, wouldn't ya?'

'Nnng,' she says.

Thought so.

She doesn't utter a sound as I dish up the roo. Stays sitting against the wall, watching the calendar, watching her fingers. I think, maybe she's hot and that's why she keeps her back against the wall. These undergrounds don't look like much from the outside but get inside them on a hot day and it's like ya just stepped into a fridge and these walls, they can be like ice packs to a sweating back. But then she's all hunched up and around the time I open the tin of peaches her lip starts shaking, like she's shivering with cold.

I put some of the roo stew on what used to be Evie's special plate. I pad it out with some greens and sit it by her side on top of her green skirt. 'Here, this'll warm ya up,' I say to her.

'Nnng,' she says. She stares at the battery fan like she wants to eat that instead.

After tea she perks up. I spread me Desert Bar books across the kitchen table and sit down and start working out how much beer I've sold as against how much I bought to sell. Pretty soon the right-hand side of the page's full up with crosses and I have to open up one of the unprofitable beers just to keep me hand steady and when I suddenly look up and see the milk that's sitting in the coolest corner but it's still going off, not because I can't afford to buy more but cos I can't afford the trip to the store, I'm about to throw the damn books against the wall when I hear, 'Nnng.'

It's Ruby. She's up and alive and standing at me elbow; I see she's taken some of the roo stew cos there's this bit of brown trickling down the side of her mouth. There's a pea wedged between her two front teeth and I see this cos she stares at me with her mouth gaping open before bending down over me figures.

Like I've always said, a day without conversation is a day in hell. I'd offer her some of me beer but it's the last one I've got, there's only the Desert Bar stash after this. But looking at her eyes, I reckon she doesn't need a drink. What she needs is a good bath, and I showed her the tank on the first day but she didn't look none too keen. So I don't mention cold water or soap to her; I just say, 'There's more in the pot if ya want it,' and 'It's cooling down outside—might get some rain,' and 'Ya hair's nice ya know, like rhubarb,' cos there's a bunch of the stuff sticking up from a vase nearby and hell, how did ya get a bird like this to talk to you?

I think for a sec I've said something she didn't take kindly to, because suddenly she's looking away from the book up to me and the rims of her eyes are looking blacker and witchier than usual if that's possible, but the bells of a thousand pokies start clanging in me head cos I know that, finally, Ruby's ready for a natter.

She says: 'This is a dumb place to stick a bar. It's never gonna take off.' She passes out.

Day ten of Ruby being here. And I reckon she's jinxed me.

Three o'clock the next day and I'm still waiting for me first customer. And it's a corker, not a scorcher, so it's perfect weather for them Volvo tourists like the ones I had stop on the road a little way up, reverse, swing their legs over the side of the car and ask me for a cold one. You'd reckon it was a tropical paradise if ya saw this weather we're having cos overhead the sky's bright and blue as Evie's eyes but there's this nice breeze coming across the desert and it's making the grasses dance. Normally looking at that I feel happy, but today it's rubbing salt into the wound.

And so's Ruby, sitting a few metres away under the carport. She's sitting cross-legged on the concrete and she's got all these coloured cards spread out in front of her like a fan and she's got one eye on them and the other on me. And it's the one day she rouses herself from the dead and comes out to watch me business, and there's nothing to watch.

She can watch me polishing the glasses, that's what. 'This is something I never had to do at the Standard,' I joke to her, for meself. 'Wipe off the insects.' The glasses are full of the buggers, like me bar's on wheels been driving through the desert with a four-sided windscreen. There's red dust all over the counter too, over the photos of me five-minute mates. I dust them down, run me sponge over the camera lens. I lift it to me eye and point it at Ruby.

But she's gone past being a five-minute mate. And I don't wanna take no chances with these photos, cos me chipboard noticeboard's jack full of photos of folks who didn't believe in me and what happens if I take a photo of this sheila with a nasty look on her face and the next day she turns round and says, 'You were right and I was wrong, Doug. This Desert Bar's gonna be a huge success,' and then she up and leaves? What happens then? When I'm famous and standing in front of them TV cameras and saying, 'This person said I'd fall flat on me face, and this person, and this one here . . .' and I point at Ruby. Isn't that like taking ya fame from someone's misfortune?

That's not to say plenty of people haven't done the same to me. And if any of them council blokes preening and sandpapering the highway back there hears about the Desert Bar and decides he might pop in for a beer one day, I'm not sure I won't put an upside-down glass on me head and tell him, 'Bar's shut.' But thinking about it all in this way makes me feel warmer towards Ruby. When I look round and see she's stopped with the cards and she's smoking another one of them big white cigarettes I yell out, 'Wanna join me for a soft drink?' cos here I am with about ten litres of raspberry lemonade and I haven't served a kid in weeks.

But she's going off into space again.

It's when she smokes and does that that I stare at the beautiful burnt land to the point on the horizon where the road starts. I wait for that semi that's gonna come and take Ruby off me hands for good. Couple of times that arvo, as she's woken up and gone to sleep and woken up to her cards again, I think I see that semi sailing towards me like a red steam engine. Or a blue one, or a green one—but today's a bad day. And on bad days I see lots of vehicles coming towards me that never actually arrive.

It's been a day in hell, with or without conversation. That night I'm sitting at the kitchen table flicking through this scrapbook I keep that's got all the things from the past I value. It's got Evie's favourite recipe in it, Cold Wallaby Rolls, but on page nine it's also got recipes from the bistro at the Standard and page ten is all stuck up with coasters and on page eleven, winking up at me before I can close the book shut, is the Standard's certificate of business registration that I whipped off the wall the day I left.

It made a beaut template. The copy's outside in the carport, pinned to me UV-protection shadecloth, but I can see it flapping in the breeze.

Suddenly I'm tired.

Ruby's sitting against the wall of the loungeroom. She's almost looking nice. All the skins she's peeled off during her time here, she's started to put back on again. She's even taken the ring out of her nose. And her lips are ruby red.

She can't leave. She can't—I didn't get one conversation out of her.

Them cards of hers are spread in front of her and she's trying to focus on them. The calendar's proving a distraction, obviously—I put it onto March, the water-melon. I was trying to think positive. I say to her, 'You're a fortune teller or something aren't ya, Ruby?'

'Nnng.'

'Then predict my future. Tell me what's gonna happen with this bar of mine.'

She stares at me a sec. Then she bends her head down over the cards and starts shuffling; she spreads the cards, all of them big and flat as cockroaches, across the floor and some of them she faces up to her and some of them down and she doesn't say a word.

In the end it's the Grim Reaper card I don't like, but she's more baffled by one with a goat and a loaf of bread. She stares at it a moment.

I think she's fallen asleep like that, with her chin pushing into her knee, but suddenly up comes her head. There's this look of foreboding in her eyes. 'The cards say this was a bad place to set up a bar,' she says. 'It's never gonna take off.'

'Say cheese,' I tell her.

I've got the Polaroid pointed at Ruby before she can even smile.

When it's good and dry, I get a black pen and write in the space underneath it: *Another satisfied customer.* I put it in me pocket. When the sun comes up, I'll go outside and pin it to the chipboard with the rest of the photos. I might even write the same thing on all of them—who'll know the difference?

I'm never gonna have to show them to any TV cameras.

AVENUE PACTHOD

Modigliani

96

BREATHE A WORD

Christopher Cyrill

Arrabella lives in an avenue in Fitzroy. After Dog left she moved into the living room and slept on a sofa bed. She let their bedroom out to single, non-smoking women. Her latest boarder leaves cellophane and tinsel sweet wrappers on the living room table. Arrabella sweeps the wrappers into her hand and crushes them into a loose ball. She touches her left shoulder and imagines that Dog is standing behind her.

Dog lives in a boarding house in Notting Hill Gate. One room. Shared bathroom. Coil of heat. He works as a bartender at the Devonshire Arms. He takes a bottle opener down to the cellar during the bottling up. Sometimes Fran comes to meet him, his hands sticky with beer, his boots stained in the shape of an unknown continent. Each night the beer spillage, the overflow of wine, redraws the maps on his boots.

A chessboard sits on the edge of the bar. White has captured the black knight and three pawns while black has captured a pawn and a bishop. The captured pieces lie in a box beside the board. With one move the black queen could checkmate the white king but all the pieces are glued to the board and the board is stained and rotting, the pieces chipped, the black king haloed with salt.

Arrabella lies on the sofa bed and can hear the boarder humming in the shower.

Dog lies alone with his hand on his semi-erect penis. He listens to the movement of people in the boarding house, hears the bathroom door shut and knows that the South African has gone for his first joint. He hears the laughter of the Sydney sisters next door, the land-lady talking in her loud gin whispers. The visitors being buzzed in. The toilet flush. The click of the TV.

—*picked up last pay cheque from the Dev'. Pulled a last bitter with a good head, made a g & t and said my goodbyes. F was out. Sank a quick Newca Brown and walked, down Pembridge onto Portobello, past a lean busker outside the Sun 'n' Splenda, the spill of crowd wide-eyed from a cinema, past a shopfront covered in newspaper with an OPEN sign on the door, another shopfront with a wine glass and a walking stick in front of a black curtain. From there to here. Into an alleyway off Talbot, an old man sleeping in a box, the owner's BMW, the back entrance of the Red Eagle. Knocked and Tony let me in, black hands the size of stop signs, mouth full of Tic-Tacs. Lights hit me like flames. I take this booth and Tone buys two house doubles and comes over and hands me one and says 'Here's to it,' and we shoot and my eyes start to water but I keep it down and get him to sign the back of my journal and he writes 'Here's to it. Good luck, Tone,' and he goes off to do the door. Sit in this booth now, 6.43 with a Newca Brown, last bender on my last night in London, keeping this journal as my thread, my trail of breadcrumbs home. Tomorrow, the arch, the tower, the graveyard.*

Remember Modigliani, 'Your real duty is to save your dream.'

Corinne makes three pounds an hour and twenty pounds a night from tips. Americans tip for no reason. She is curt with French customers and notices that only the men ask about the specials. Englishmen never make eye contact. She hides the money she is saving for her ticket home in a tampon box.

Dog waits outside the showers on the second floor. He waits for Corinne. He does not know why. He has stolen one of her letters from the mail table in the foyer of the boarding house. He cannot read French but recognises the words 'mort' and 'cafe' and 'fleurs'.

Esteban rides his moped past the Church of St Christopher and along Avenue Emile Zola. He stops at a bar.

Dog wonders why women take so long in the shower.

Arrabella writes a letter to Dog. She addresses the envelope to John Collie and in the letter she writes, 'I need to know when/if you are coming home.'

PUB FICTION

Esteban drinks beer every night. He lives on Avenue du Marechal de Tassigny and each evening on his way back from his renovator's job he buys two six packs of Heineken from the petrol station. He can only eat when he is drunk, otherwise he has no appetite. As he drinks he rehearses conversations with Corinne. He tells her that no one will ever be good enough for his mother but he doesn't care any more, and now he has full-time work they can afford to live together. By his ninth beer he is talking aloud, his hands conducting the conversation. Arrabella thinks, 'She has eyes like chocolates.'

—*straight down Talbot to Porchester onto Gloucester, saw a man covered with a blanket in a doorway, red hair, tuft of his goatee dyed blue. Beggar with a baby swaddled in newspaper, took a pound coin from my payslip and gave it to her. Man with a neck like a llama. Where's the busker singing Streets of London? Too bright in here, too full. Two men, Spanish I guess by their accents, sip pints and watch the World Cup. Baggio slips his marker and dances around the full-back and curves one wide.*

Remembering the last World Cup, waking from A, reluctant to leave her body, her talcum powder morning smell, her knees drawn up to her stomach. Watched Cameroon lose to England in extra time, cup after cup of coffee, running out of cigs with fifteen minutes to go. Move on.

Dog signs his letters to Arrabella 'Always,' but he omits the stroke in the middle of the 'A'. He also writes XXXOOO at the bottom of each page.

Corinne sits at the edge of the bath. She says 'Hail Marys' and the prayer to the Virgin that does not fail.

She prays that the Australian is not waiting outside the door.

Dog is growing a beard. He rarely irons his Taylor-Walker shirt which is part of his uniform. His hands shake so he often spills drinks on customers. He steals pound coins from the till or overcharges drunk customers and feeds the jukebox. His favourite songs are 3601, 8205, 8514. When he thinks of Arrabella his left eye twitches. He hopes that one day Corinne will come into the bar and he will give her free drinks and offer her cigarettes and she will wait while he bottles up and turns the chairs and cleans and stacks the glasses and they'll walk home together and keep the gravity between their bodies until they reach the landing of the second floor.

Estaban calculates that if he gave up drinking for four weeks he could afford the trip to London. He thinks of the Australian who stands outside the door of the shower. He imagines the man as close to thirty years old with spectacles a little too large for his face, his hair in a side part.

A man buys Dog a drink. Dog puts the change in his pocket. The managers allow him a pint after work and whatever the customers buy him if he receipts it. Usually he drinks gin and lemonade while he works, or vodka. He stops drinking about an hour before closing time, when the husband and wife who run the pub come down to chat with the regulars and to handle any of the stragglers. The husband likes to ring the bell.

Arrabella can't decide what to wear. The boarder is

already dressed and is stuffing a cigarette. The boarder doesn't like clubs so they're going to see a band at the Espy, maybe a pizza afterwards. Arrabella would rather stay at home and drink wine and get stoned and eat M&Ms. Maybe order a pizza. The Espy reminds her of Dog and she wonders if she'll end up sitting on the bench and crying, or making a drunk long-distance call.

A man tries to put a ten pound note down Corinne's blouse and she tips a bowl of soup into his lap. She then breaks a plate on the floor and walks out of the restaurant. On the way home she decides that she will never return to Esteban and considers moving to Amsterdam. She realises that she is still wearing her apron as she walks up the stairs of the boarding house. She enters her room and undresses and wraps a towel around her body and takes her toiletries bag to the shower.

Dog thinks of buying Arrabella a present from Portobello Markets as he sips his Newcastle Brown Ale after closing time. The wife, Fran, wants to talk to him alone. She says that money is missing from the till. She is sure it is not him but asks him to keep an eye on the other staff, especially when they make change for the jukebox. Dog begins to rub her breasts while she talks. He rubs them through the silk of her purple blouse. He kisses her neck. She unzips her skirt. He kisses the inside of her thighs. He pulls down her panties. She unbuttons her blouse. Dog says, Don't breathe a word. He says it as a threat. He fingers her and makes her kiss his fingers. Then he stops and continues to drink.

—from there to here. The Pardoner. Down Edgeware, past a synagogue, onto Connaught, Albion, back onto

Bayswater. I come a half-circle. The gates of Hyde, the shadow of a couple in the window of an apartment. A bus with a flat tyre, piss smelling bus stop. Marble Arch, downstairs, the priest on the elevator descending, Emmanuel Beart's face on the cover of Paris Match, a Tarantino interview, ticket, inspectors talking to a fare dodger, through the steel shutters onto the platform, a tunnel sealed with a mosaic of brick, a wedge of night sky, the tube to Tottenham Court Road. In the train the refined distances between people and my reflection in the window, the one constant in the dark tunnel, journey so fast it seems still, behind me four old ladies discussing some play they have seen. Out onto the platform into the first pub the street gave up. Nameless, dead empty pub, one drink and out onto the street again.

I found an empty table and put my journal down and bought a shot of bourbon and a Newca Brown. A scimitar hangs above the bar. The red-eyed bartender is keeping a book with Brazil at 7–4. Outside a dosser with a beard like a camel. Man at the corner table, lips pursed as he writes an airmail letter, wears a hat with a fish embroidered on it, sneaking the cap of a flask in his pocket, sly sips and fugitive measures. Outside a woman wolfing down a Big Mac, tongue on her fingertips for the dripping mayonnaise and two men playing backgammon, the run and the roll and the black and the white, the smell of fried sausages and the house bitter. Ale froth settles in hexagons on the inside of my bottle and perhaps soon the coupling of bodies and fists or headlong to the off-licence.

The fish-hat takes a plate of chips to the corner and I remember other evenings, another country, the meat fawn in turmeric, pasta salad, tin-foil potatoes and the last of the longnecks deep in the icemelt, the labels floating like abandoned sails. The click, click, click of my father's slides; the Empire State, the Grand Canyon, the G.M. plant and the boss, then Dad with an unnamed woman in fake stockades at Disneyworld. Two slides later the pair of them encircled in Mickey Mouse's big paws, eating snow cones. From there to here, a car leaves the driveway, moving, always moving, a sack of potatoes in the garage, their long weedy eyes poking through the hessian, the Smirnoff bottles out for recycling, a baseball glove on my sixteenth, the hire of a Commodore when I got my licence, Mum at the door after a dance with one shoe in her hand, Arrabella's bones and the geography of desire, tongue deep into her scapula yet throughout, my impotence, the god and the faith but the inability to pray. A letter regretting to inform me, my inheritance, and before I left, dusting off trays of dark windows disordered, a narrative of boxes random, loose, bear each moment, each gesture to the light, and Arrabella's eyes.

Corrine opens the bathroom door and Dog is standing before her. She hears the Sydney sisters come giggling down the stairs and stops herself from spitting in Dog's face. One of the sisters barks at Dog. Corinne walks past him.

Dog and Fran masturbate in front of each other.

The boarder blows smoke in Arrabella's direction.

On the way home Dog stops at an off-licence. It is past eleven. He looks at the camera above the shopkeeper and makes a gesture with his shoulder towards the fridge. The shopkeeper nods and Dog puts down five pounds and takes a packet of chewing gum from a rack. Out of the camera's view he walks to the fridge and puts two bottle of ale in the sleeves of his jacket. He nods at the shopkeeper. The shopkeeper nods back. Dog walks out.

Esteban sees a man at the bar who looks exactly like the Dog he has imagined. Esteban drinks and sees himself smashing a bottle over the man's face. He thinks of the confetti of glass, the man's eyes filling with blood, the drinkers stunned, motionless, the door swinging shut behind him. He walks out of the bar. He starts his moped.

—didn't check street names. Don't feel lost. Think I'm a bus away from home. Got in before the bell, finishing up. Is it worse to not have what you want or to not know what you want? Tomorrow, the tower, the arch, the graveyard.

Arrabella begins a letter to Dog and then crumples it up and tries to phone him. The boarder knocks on the door of her bedroom.

Corinne reads the letter over and over again. She forgets she has the bath running.

Dog's not home, one of the Sydney sisters says.

Esteban swallows his tongue. A spoke severs his Achilles.

Dog gets to the second floor and feels his lungs tighten. He inhales ventolin. He looks at the carpet beneath his feet. The carpet is stained with water and above him water drips from the body of a light bulb.

A man sitting outside a cafe and drinking Heineken sees the whole thing. The impact. The somersault.

Dog tries to remember, tries to retrace his steps.

EXHIBITIONISTS

Paul Hastie

'**L**ook out!' A small Fiat pulled up in front of us. Rod chuckled to himself. 'She's here.'

A short man in a red suit got out and rushed around to the passenger side, releasing impossibly long legs. Above them, a dark-haired girl in gold lycra leggings and a rubber bra.

'Oh, I don't know, really,' she was saying, looking at the gallery. The drone of opening-night chatter filled the air. Rod went over and introduced himself.

'Hi mate,' said the guy, 'I'm Bruno. This is Tonya. What's the score?'

'It's simple,' Rod told Tonya, 'I'll put on the music— it's *To Sir with Love*—and all you do is go up to the Director and—'

'Director?' she said, 'What Director?'

'The Director of the gallery,' Rod began. Tonya turned to Bruno.

'No, really, I *really* don't feel good about it.'

'But it's gonna be great!' insisted Rod. Tonya stared at him.

'Didn't tell me it was mixed, did you?'

'Mixed?' gasped Rod.

'Sexes,' said Bruno, 'Tonya doesn't like it.' He braced one of her shoulders with a hairy-backed hand. 'Relax, Tonya, okay? This is just some dumb art crowd. You'll never see them again.'

'Yeah,' said Rod, 'they'll just think you're some kind of performance artist or something.'

'What'ya mean THINK?'

'Look, Tonya,' said Bruno, trying to placate her, 'just treat it like any other gig.'

'Fucking sicko!' She glared at Rod. 'What do you think I am? A PIECE OF MEAT?'

Bruno sighed. 'Sorry, mate, she won't do it now, no way.' His hands were heavy lumps in the pockets of his jacket.

'And you wanted jelly too, didn't you?' said Tonya. She turned on her heels and made for the car door.

'I didn't say nothing about no jelly,' pleaded Rod. 'I just wanted an everyday strip. Please?'

She shook her head. 'Let's go, Bruno.' Rod leapt between Tonya and the car.

'A hundred and fifty!' he yelled. 'Two hundred! Please! Tonya!'

She stopped, briefly calculating, then again shook her head. Bruno turned his palms out and shrugged. In seconds they were gone. Rod guzzled from a bottle of wine, stripperless.

'Shit! That was meant to be my performance. I wanted to do something meaningful with my life!'

Almost immediately, a guy in an Oasis T-shirt came up and said, 'Hi Rod!'

'Oh, hi Eacham,' he said in a dejected tone.

'I just heard you were going to have a *stripper* appearing here.' As if he was talking about paint removal.

'Yeah. She wouldn't do it.'

Eacham twitched and cooed happily, wetting his lips, which were nailed down by white pimples either side of his mouth. 'What's it all about anyway? Don't you think it's rather, er, shall I say . . . banal? Not to mention *passé*? Don't you recall our lecture last week on the failure of performance art?'

'This isn't about art,' said Rod.

'Oh, dear, I *am* in the wrong place!' Eacham turned to me, hand thrust quick as a knackery bolt. I supposed I had to shake the sweaty thing. 'Hi, History Major at UTS,' he said, frown muscles well trained.

'Danny,' I said cautiously.

'Oh, is this your old friend, Rod?' Eacham stifled a giggle. Rod slapped my shoulder.

'Bullshit, this guy's no friend of mine.'

'Never seen the arsehole before in my life,' I said.

Eacham gurgled uncertainly. 'Is that an anal joke? You know, Lacan writes that the anus is the gateway—

'My gateway's clogged,' I said, 'I need some water.'

I escaped the awfulness of Eacham and went back inside the gallery, now desperate to get out of this art scene. Maybe go drinking at Yuk's club up the Cross, reminisce about Rooty Hill High. I wanted to seize Rod and leave immediately, but being a persistent sort of loser, he was still scouting for strippers.

'Sue, please, it would mean a lot to me,' he implored

a girl with long black hair. She folded her arms reso-
lutely, sizing him up.

'Means a lot to me too, Rod. My fucking reputation,
that is.'

'I'll give you $250.'

'No way! My parents are here!'

Rod was wilting. He pulled at his hair and a chunk
came out.

'Look, I agree with you on principle,' she continued,
'but fucked if I'm doing a striptease at my own gradu-
ation show! I mean, get fucking real!'

Rod needed a distraction, and he needed it quick. I
said the first thing that came to mind—'Let's go to Yuk's.'

Rod's nose twitched. 'He there tonight?'

'It's Friday. I'll give him a call. Now, wait here, and
for fuck's sake don't ask anyone else, or you'll cop a
harassment charge.'

'Ask him if he can get us a stripper.'

'Rod, it's over!' I tried to get it into his head. 'The
fucking people are going to their fucking homes!'

'Just ask him!'

From the phone at the club, Yuk predictably told me
that despite being mates, he was but a lowly bouncer and
was in no position to ask the boss for any wacky favours.
'But youse should come up and get free drinks if youse
want.'

It sounded like a plan. When I returned, Rod was
talking with his girlfriend Rowie and co-exhibitor Sue.

'Heard about the no-go go-go?' I said to Rowie.

'Yeah.' She smiled, wide brown eyes rolling towards
Rod. 'He knows there's no way I'm doing it.'

It was tricky to distract Rod from his urgent but
hopeless search for a potential stripper in the crowd. I
had to all but slap his face.

'Let's go to Yuk's. Free drinks, eh? Not to mention the floorshow.'

'What floorshow?' Sue asked.

'It's the crappiest club in town,' Rod said despondently. Behind him, Eacham arched his head closer.

'I'll come and check it out,' said Sue.

'Yeah,' said Rowie, 'let's do it.'

Dull and searchless, Eacham said, 'uh, okay then!' when we made to step on.

'As if he's been invited,' said Rowie.

'Don't worry, we'll lose him,' whispered Sue.

Everyone was glad to leave the gallery. We took the winding streets, through the flats, up to the Cross. Eacham trailed behind, trying to impress Sue with harrowing tales of his therapy.

'They wanted me on double Stelazine, but it gives me the hives. I thought I'd give positive affirmations a proper go. It works for mother.'

We came to the start of the Big Bad Half-Kilometre. The club where Yuk worked was near the giant Coke sign.

'That's it,' I said, nodding towards the shop with the huge neon heart and the screaming sign, 'LIVE NUDE GIRLS!' Eacham's tone rose and he whined, 'What, here? Really?', titillated with fear. Yuk was out on the street, spruiking. He was twenty-one, but looked at least fifty. His fat gut faced us.

'Free show! C'mon guys and girls, we got the seven wonders of the world upstairs, featuring the Dee-lightful Delilah, and she does—hey, Rod! Danny! Rowie! Maaaaaate! Better not go charging youse now, eh?'

'Hah!' Rowie said, 'You said it was free, you rip-off merchant!'

'Lovely as ever,' Yuk said. 'Who's yer mates?'

Rowie introduced him to the others. 'This is Sue. Sue, Yuk.' She turned to Eacham. 'And this is F—uh, Eacham.'

'Pleased to meet you,' Eacham stuttered, unsure of which hand to shake. Yuk had 'HATE' tattooed on the knuckles of both hands, the funny bugger. Always had to be the extremist.

'All right, all right,' he said, waving us off, 'go on upstairs. I'm on the bar in ten minutes, I'll see youse then, eh?'

We wandered in, up the mirror-walled staircase, punctuated by flashing bead-lights.

'Sort of eighties tacky version of deco, isn't it?' said Eacham. We all ignored him. The swirling red lights reflected infinitely in mirrors leading up to the second floor.

The club was comprised of a bar at the back, eight rows of chairs and an aisle leading up to a mirror-lined stage. A video played on one wall. A girl, her cheeks plump with cockmeat. A moog bass thumped throughout. When Yuk appeared at the bar, I went straight up to see him.

'So how'd the bloody art thing go?' he roared.

I told him about Rod's latest scheme, the art gallery and the aborted performance. He relayed it to two of his customers, and their laughter swept the bar like piss down a urinal. Yuk's boss, a fattish shorty with a loose beard, cackled as he counted a fat wad of fifties.

'What do you think I am?' Yuk shouted, 'a piece of meat?'

'Well, actually I did,' spluttered one toothless guy with a very hairy nose. They went into hysterics again. Across the bar, Rod was pouting. He must have known we were talking about him. Yuk turned back to me, still laughing.

'Next time, mate, give us some warning. For $250 we coulda got him two bloody strippers an' a fucking python! Anyhow, drink up. Just wave some money at me so's it looks like ya paying.'

I gave him a twenty and he handed me a tray with five stubbies on it, the twenty tucked underneath one of them.

'Come back later,' he said quietly, 'I might have a bit of a surprise.' He winked and returned to the bar.

I went back to our table and sidled in next to Rod and Rowie, chuckling to myself as I noticed that Eacham was stuck with a crashed-out biker next to him. The 'digger was collapsing onto his shoulder. Yuk offered to move him, but Rod said, 'Where's the fun in that?'

'Let him squirm,' whispered Rowie, and we all agreed.

The next act was beginning. Like the movies, you can tell by the music. Gary Glitter's *Rock and Roll*, the only good song all night. We were in the second row, ten feet from centre stage, and the blonde seemed to step straight out of a mirror. She looked bored and mechanical, pouting and shaking her tits as she worked her way down to a G-string. She finished her act efficiently, then disappeared into the mirrors in a white vinyl coat.

'Look,' said Sue, pointing towards Eacham. The bikie was sound asleep on his shoulder, and Eacham was squirming, sneering with disapproval.

'Doesn't look too comfortable.'

'Probably got a hard-on.'

Xandra, the next act, was energetic and highly skilled at smiling. After a sultry dance and some daring gymnastics, she disappeared and the lights brightened slightly.

Scowling, Eacham leaned over the unconscious Gravedigger.

'This is so sick! I can't help feeling sorry for these poor women! Just look at their shattered lives!'

'You don't get out much, do you?' said Sue, guzzling one drink and grabbing another, her long black hair now saturated by a missed drink.

'At what price human life?' spluttered Eacham, his eyes wide, demanding an answer. We were all too far gone to bother replying.

'And now, here she is!' boomed Yuk's voice over the PA. 'The star of the show. The dee-licious, dee-lightful, Dee-lilah!'

To minimal applause, a dark figure in a leopard skin teddy strutted onto the stage.

'Now, *those* are bazookas!' shouted Rod, more than loud enough for Eacham's ears.

'Silicone Valley,' said Sue. 'It amazes me how those tits point straight ahead like that.'

'She can actually dance, too,' said Rowie, who must have been on rowies to think that. On stage, Delilah spread her ass cheeks wide, beautifully accompanied by *Walking on Sunshine*. Eacham shook his head morosely.

'Hey, Danny!' Yuk was leaning over my shoulder. 'Bossman's pissed off for an hour. Come here.' He led me across the bar to a back room. It was empty apart from a medium-sized desk, a chair and a Super Mario calendar. Yuk closed the door behind us, slipped on the latch and rummaged in a desk drawer.

'Check this out.'

I expected to see a little baggie and some syringes, but what Yuk held in his hands truly shocked me. An A4 piece of paper. A pastel pink and peach sunset scene. He shuffled on his feet and looked at me expectantly.

'Well? What d'ya reckon?'

I was speechless.

'It's a fucking watercolour, aint it?'

'What,' I said, '*you* did this?'

'It's got me fucking name on the bottom, hasn't it?'

I looked close to see *Robert Yukovic* scrawled in the corner of the page. 'You don't have to get defensive,' I said, 'I'm just—'

'What?'

'Surprised. Nice—er—colours.'

Yuk beamed at the drawing proudly. 'Gotta stay here all night. Doing this shit keeps me entertained. You think it's good?'

'You'll have to show it to Rod. He's the artist.'

Yuk backed away. 'Hey, don't get funny! Just wanted to show ya, that's all.'

'I had no idea, Yuk. You're a marvel!'

'Yeah, well, I got the idea after watching this show about Prince Charles.'

When we walked back into the Club room, it was immediately apparent that our crowd were louder than they should have been.

'It was a brawl. Fuck me dead!' said Yuk.

'Piss off, you wimpy pus-ball!' a woman's voice screamed, 'I'll kill you!'

Yuk dived into the chaos. I drew closer, and saw him having a hard time holding Delilah back. She was clawing with rage—at Eacham!

'You miserable slimy dickhead!'

Eacham was a falling-apart-crying-man-on-his-knees. The stoned biker stirred from his sleep and started itching and clapping. Must have thought this place had a really unique act, the attack-stripper.

'What the fuck's going on?' I asked Rod, but he was gripped in an urgent search for a roll of film.

'This is it!' he yelled. 'It's the fucking performance! It makes sense now!'

Sue and Rowie were making for the bar, spitting, shrieking and laughing. *Walking on Sunshine* kept playing. The guys at the bar were ripped and oblivious. Delilah was livid, slapping Eacham's face. For a second, I considered getting involved.

'What happened?' I asked Sue and Rowie.

'She was starting up a lap dance,' said Sue, 'tits wobbling, and he—'

'No!' I covered my ears. 'He didn't!'

'Slobbered all over her! She started karate-chopping him.'

'Maybe he was so pissed he thought she liked him,' I suggested.

'Can you get that pissed?' said Sue. No-one could say.

'You look,' Delilah screamed at Eacham, 'you pay to fucking look, right, you little prick! Don't you ever fucking touch what you can't pay for! Not fucking ever, not unless you're paying!' She looked him up and down. 'No, not even then, you ugly creep!' She drew up her elbow, ready to deliver another blow.

'Now, Delilah,' Yuk said, 'hold up!'

She spat on Eacham's face, then dropped him with a high kick to the chest. Rod loaded the film into his camera.

'Man,' he said to me. 'This is bee-yew-tiful!'

'Jeez, he'll need some therapy after this,' laughed Rowie.

Eacham rolled around, shielding his face with his arms.

'Hey guys,' called Yuk, who seemed to be restraining Delilah only for our benefit. 'He with youse or what?'

I looked to Rowie, who was watching it all from the seats. She shook her head.

'No way,' shouted Rod, snapping furiously from every angle. 'Fucking history, man. *Passé.*'

'Right then, Delilah, he's all yours.' Yuk released Delilah, then turned to me with a wink. 'I'm off to practice me pastel washes.'

CERTAINTY

Anne Maree Weatherall

That Johnny. When he look at me sometimes—his eyes are like an animal. He looks at me as if he means to keep me. He can do it with his eyes but mostly he don't bother. I tell him, 'You can look at me with those diamond blue eyes and keep me there like a roo trapped by headlights.' He just laughs and looks away. I try to walk away from a fella like that. I try. A man like that, quiet, broody, mad at times, not gossiped about. I try to walk but my legs are stuck. He walks away from me instead. I follow. A little way behind, trying to catch up naturally, but it's impossible; I have to run like a child.

'Where you goin' Johnny?'

'Shops.'

'Can I come too?' I say, not trying to be cute, just wanting to be with him.

He turns and smiles right at me, broadly, laughs at my bravado.

The door opened. A boy stood looking at Aggie.

'Is Johnny there?' she asked nervously.

'Nup,' he said, looking past her at the car. Two little girls behind him took off down the hallway calling, 'Mum, Mum, there's a lady at the door.'

'Is that your car?' the boy said.

'Nah, work car.' She smiled. He didn't smile back. A big bearded man appeared up the hallway.

'You after Johnny? He'd be down the pub. I know you, don't I?'

'Yeah.'

'You work for that community health mob?'

'Yeah. My name's Aggie.'

'Come in love. I'm James. You want a cuppa? Or is it just Johnny you want?' He gave a big hearty laugh.

'Well maybe a quick one, I'm on work time.'

'Sit down there. This is my wife Rita. This here is Aggie, she lookin' for Johnny. Cup of tea eh?' Rita smiled and got up to make the tea. 'Hard man to catch on payday. Did you check the Kurrajong?'

'No, I just was on my way back to work and I thought I'd drop in.'

'Rita is Johnny's sister.' He nodded towards her. 'Look at this 'ere, from prisoners' aid.' A big carton of tinned goodies sat on the sideboard.

'D'you just get out of prison?'

'Gawd no, I've been out for seven years.'

Rita laughed and shook her head, said something Aggie didn't understand. She had Johnny's sparkling eyes and masses of thick curly hair, pulled back in a scrunchie. Aggie took an instant shine to Johnny's family.

'So what you got?' James asked Aggie. 'You got coffee, nappies?'

'No, not me.' She was beginning to think he'd got her mixed up with someone else, so she explained that she visited people after they were discharged from hospital. 'Got diabetic needles though.'

'Rita can use them.' James said, happy to have got down to tin tacks.

'Gotta do it here,' Rita said pointing to her stomach, 'twice a day.'

Rita pulled a smoke out of her bum bag. She said something, running her words together so that they clicked and clacked, like singing, low murmuring. If it hadn't been for the extra smoke she pulled out and offered Aggie she never would have understood what she had meant. They smoked while James talked about a Trifecta he'd won recently.

'And I only boxed it at the last minute 'cause George came in and gave me the extra six dollars.'

Aggie grew restless thinking about Johnny. He was close, maybe at the corner pub. She'd been dreaming about him. In the dream, he walked straight up to her, and kissed her with such belief. That kiss, in the dream, the one with all the suction and integrity—that was the kiss she was after.

Heartbeat, breathless, Aggie felt like a drink, but didn't think she'd get away with it today. No control. She had to have control, pace herself, otherwise she wouldn't make it to the end of the shift. Nightshifts were shorter, she could have a couple of cans, knock off and finish her drinking at the pub. Some shifts they'd do deliveries, bulk needles to out-of-it customers, and buy a can at a time. They were the alcoholic section of the team. They had a pub run as well as the usual deliveries.

'You'll find him at the Kurrajong, or the Shaky. That's where he'd be today, with Kevin,' James said, like it was a dead cert. Like the races he was having a bet on. Yep, this horse will shit in.

The Kurrajong looked dead; there were a few people bent over pool tables, and a couple at the bar. Aggie drove to The Rose, same thing, a quiet midday death. She tried the Erko, then the Shakespeare—nobody, nothing. It wasn't a particularly warm day but she felt slightly sweaty. Sometimes it was panic, other times it was excitement, she couldn't tell them apart. She wanted it quickly, flying, ghostlike, now. Parking the big work van was becoming cumbersome. She fought the lack of power steering and reversed fast. Maybe he went back home. They said they'd make him wait there if he went back home.

'Did you find him?'

'No.'

'He hasn't been back, he's over Redfern drinking somewhere, have you tried Aunty Daisy's?'

'He'll be here, don't you worry about that. Kevin's birthday. He's in for two flagons.' Aunty Daisy spoke with absolute certainty about everything. She stood with her small hands on her large hips looking towards the top of the mission, and even further, as if she were waiting for something more than the flagons. Aggie looked too, copying the fierce look that Aunty Daisy often had in her eyes.

'You lookin' for Johnny?' piped up ol' Edgar. 'He's up the top drinkin'.'

Well, you never heard so many certain people in your life. Aggie had been up the top several times, around the park, the theatre, all the spots. No Johnny. This was wearing her out. She just wanted to sit down and get drunk. Better still, go home and get a good sleep; all this running around wasn't making her look too good anyway. And work would be sending out a search party soon. She'd look out for him tomorrow, all fresh and done up a bit. It was important. She kept thinking of his smile. It was scary, what was she going to do? He'd eat her alive. She stood there a long time doing nothing, saying nothing, waiting for something or someone to save her from any decision. Sonny, Edgar's nephew, who used to be a footy star, handed the poor girl a longneck and watched the bony thing swallow half the bottle in one long swig. He started to grimace, took his bottle back, looked at it. 'Thirsty eh?' he said and walked away, clutching his bottle.

The sun was going down through the trees. There was a bit of a chill in the air, and that feeling that everyone better knock off drinking, or go to the pub, or fall down.

'Puttin' in for a carton?'

'VB.'

'Half 'n' half Tooheys.'

'Oney got two dollar.'

'That'll do. Monty!' the short squat woman shouted, 'You ol' cunt, been suckin' on our beers all day, never put a dollar in.'

The old, old, maybe not so old man pushed his long gnarly hands through his dark greased hair, like he was gonna start singing, or at least say something smart. He felt his pocket with the other hand. It was empty. Not having the money took the smart ass right out of him. Aggie wished she'd had some money, but she'd put in her last fifteen dollars already, and was swallowing the last of the VB.

'Go on, you right ol' fella,' Betty said, seeing his strange loss of words and slapping him on his back. She often berated the ol' fella herself, but that was different, she was his niece. He'd call her some names, and then she'd call him worse and they'd go off down the club together.

'Well, we got seventeen now,' Ben said, looking at no-one in particular but catching everyone's attention.

'Gawd! Take me ten then,' Betty said. 'I expect a drink back next week.'

The young lads scooped up the money and headed off to the pub.

'Aggie, Uncle Mick wants to see you inside,' said Daisy's boy, Leon, who swore he'd never touch drink since he'd seen it kill too many of his relations. She went straight in and found Uncle sitting on one of the beds. He was drunk, looking every bit his thirty-eight years. He wore a headband and a colourful vest with the Aboriginal flag colours. He was laughing and teasing.

'You comin' with me?' he said straight out with a cheeky laugh.

Leon saw Aggie's awkwardness.

'She go with Johnny,' he stated undeniably. Which was a funny thing to say since this was only a fantasy in Aggie's mind, and she'd never gone anywhere except the shop with Johnny.

'Johnny!' Uncle said. 'Johnny! Who the fuck is Johnny? Johnny Lennon? He's dead. She can't go with him.' Then he burst into wild laughter and swallowed another mouthful of beer.

'Johnny Smith,' Leon said.

'Is that true?' Uncle waited a bit. 'Well he's not here now is he?'

Aggie could see he meant no harm and excused

herself back out to the front. The young fella told her to pay no attention, Uncle didn't mean anything by it. Aggie wasn't from around this way and wasn't related to anyone. Most thought she was lonely, mustn't have much family and were happy to look out for her as a part of the mob.

'Here comes the birthday boy,' Daisy called from fifty yards. 'C'mon ya freckly faced cunt, we got a case comin' directly. Matter a fact, you better be goin' and gettin' one yerself.' Kevin was in his Sunday best by the look of it, his hair all greased back and a button-up shirt on. Daisy turned and gave Aggie a wink. 'Look Johnny comin' there too.'

Johnny kept his eye on Aggie all the way from the top of the mish. He smiled when he saw her mad, bright dress, then shook his head, as if he was trying to keep the dark curls out of his eyes, but he was laughing to himself. She thought he looked real handsome; those features that would never change and the mouth that would never grow thin. He walked straight up to her.

'How are you?'

'Alright thanks, how's yourself?' She was feeling cockier now, more sure of herself. 'I thought you'd gone off and got married.'

'No. Not me. I'm not married,' he said. Aggie had cleverly exacted the information without embarrassing herself. He turned to go and get her a chair and her heart ached that he might not come back, but he did, briefly; got her a beer from the fridge and walked about shaking hands with people he hadn't seen in a while. Aggie sat with the girls as they planned what they might do for the rest of the evening. There was talk of going to the pub until the heavy clomping sound of running gunjies caught their attention. Chuckie Riley ducked past the girls and doubled back up the side alley. The gunjies tore past, hopeless and breathless. They looked so funny. The tall, lanky bugger lost his hat, and the short stocky one laboured along like a truck, heavy-footed, trying to get his breath and talk into the walkie-talkie, and Chuckie, he run like the wind only silent and gone. Everyone jeered and whooped as the gunjies charged past the point where they'd lost Chuckie, and then disappeared in the maze of buildings down the end of the mish. People would say 'See ya down the mish.' Aggie supposed they said that because the mission sloped down and away from the entrance. Then they might say 'goin' uptown' and that didn't neccessarily mean up as in steep, but up as in dressing up.

A blare of country music threatened to blow everyone's ear drums out as Johnny forced the volume knob back onto the broken old wireless. It hadn't worked all day. Pliers, pliers, no pliers? Knife, knife, here's a knife. That's it. Nobody minded how loud it was, as long as it was working. Patsy Kline crooned loud as the defeated gunjies plodded back up the street. Chuckie came from out the back and sat with the girls at the front fence. The gunjies looked over, and Chuckie stared straight back at them, eyes like a python, green and cold, past them, through them. The gunjies kept walking. Aggie looked over at Johnny who smiled, all pretty eyes, and then she looked at Chuckie.

'They didn't recognise you?' she asked incredulously.

'Nup. Dopey cunts.' That was all he said. He just sat sullen, watching.

'We all look alike,' Johnny said, with just a hint of disgust in his voice. He got up off the table to get another beer. 'You know there was a robbery out west once and the police came down here looking for one of the suspects.

They wanted to know if anyone knew a bloke called "Cuz".'

Aggie howled with laughter, and the girls joined in and everyone laughed until tears ran down their cheeks. Aggie laughed too long, too loud, then cried.

'Why are you so sad?' Johnny asked.

She didn't know. She was melting, fast, and the beer was helping. And there was always something to cry about. He put his arm around her and pulled her to him gently.

'C'mon now, I'll get you another drink.'

'The party's out the back,' Daisy called. Everyone filed out to the backyard, fighting their way through the rows of washing to see the birthday cake.

'Bet you didn't expect this cunt!' she said pointing to the cake. Kevin stood a little way away, shyly considering what he had to do. Someone a bit drunker got tangled in the washing and Kevin tried to get them out, everyone ducking in and out and getting tangled, Kevin hooting with laughter and still trying to avoid the cake business.

'Kevin, get here.' Daisy had him by the shirt this time. She'd lit all the candles and was smiling proudly at him. 'C'mon, my nephew, make a wish.'

He hesitated, like the only wish he had was for the cake business to be over, then blew hard at the candles. Everyone sang *Happy Birthday* and waited for big creamy chunks of cake.

Darkness fell around the group, faces singing, laughing, talking, some just staring into the flames of the fire the younger boys had lit to keep everyone warm. Aggie was charged up now and sitting up next to Johnny on the table. She'd only just got to him since she'd been singing with Kevin and his Uncle Best for the last half hour. She barely got out a word, when George came over to her.

'Sister girl, go and sit by Kevin will you, I can't stand his cryin' no more.'

True enough, Kevin was sitting by the fire, tears streaming down his face. Aggie put her arm around his shoulder, the arm with the longneck attached to it.

'What's wrong Kev?'

Kevin hiccupped and let out a sob. He went to speak then shook his head, wiped his face hard with the back of his sleeve and looked straight into Aggie's eyes. The fire burnt bright in their faces. Brown eyes 40,000 years old reflecting the fire, reflecting each other. His lips puffy and holding back a cry, holding Aggie there with his eyes, making a stand then shifting, and losing, lost. Lost. The Warumpi song came into Aggie's head:

You want to finish up. I don't want to finish up. I want to live. You want to be here tomorrow. We gotta be strong.

'I never had a birthday cake before. In all my thirty-four years, I never had a cake.' He cried into his hands.

Daisy made the last call:

'Let's go to the pub!' It was her last because she lay down near the fire almost as soon as she'd said it. Johnny hoisted her up into his arms and took her inside to bed. She was all giggles and curses. 'You can carry me to the disco. Put me down ya' big bastard. I'll show youse all how to barn dance. I will!'

Chuckie's friend Reggie had joined the group too and even though he didn't drink he echoed the call. 'Let's go to the pub!'

CERTAINTY

It was a funny time to go to the pub because nobody had any money left, but then there was nothing left to drink either so in that way it was the smartest move. That's blackfellas for you, always got hope. The group moved up the street together, feeling strong. They were a mob. Together. They'd be right. Reggie was out front as the group left the mish and walked out onto the main crossing. He pretended to be drunk and fell over on the road to the astonishment of the whitefellas pulled up in their cars. Gee it was funny. It was the first smile on Chuckie's face all night. When he smiled, there was no trace of anger. The rest of the group hammed it up for the whitefellas and laughed themselves silly as they regrouped down the side street.

The pub was chockers, the dance floor empty. The DJ played the latest hip hop and rap songs. The mob marched in, spread out, some to the pool table, some to the quiet side, the women over near the dance floor. Everyone stood back as Johnny did one of his fancy dances. Aggie begged him to dance with her.

'No, that's it, I don't dance all night. Here, dance with Kevin.' He dragged them together and then walked off over to the pool table. Kevin was showing her how to 'dirty dance' and she only went along with it because Kevin was so insistent, but then she fancied they might even look good. Anyhow, everytime Aggie looked around, Johhny was looking the other way. She felt sure he was watching. He was crafty alright.

Out of nowhere, Kevin's ex-girlfriend appeared and slammed him a beauty, knocking him to the ground. Then she was gone again. In these cases you either make a quick exit or fight. Aggie walked over and sat with

Johnny's sister Ronny, as if nothing had happened. Kevin brushed himself off and came over to the two women.

'What you go and do that for?' Kevin asked Aggie. Ronny grabbed her arm and they laughed hysterically.

'She never hit you Kevin,' Ronny said, seeing him getting upset. 'It was that Mary Jane there.'

'Well c'mon then let's dance.' Kevin reached over to Aggie.

'No way, I'm not going to get killed over a dance.'

'Least of all over a dance with you Kevin Egan, eh Aggie?' Ronny elbowed Aggie and laughed herself silly. Kevin gave them both a quizzical look, and went off in search of another partner.

Johnny was playing doubles now. Aggie watched his partner, Barbie Bourke. Drunken jealousy is much worse than normal jealousy. It's got no sense to it. It's pure and stupid. It smells, it breathes, it kills. Even though the grog had taken its toll on Barbie and she was as drunk as a skunk, she could still play deadly pool. Her eyes were sharp and serious, still beautiful, and her rough beaten cheeks didn't look too bad with her thick curly hair falling around her face. Tiny, bony thing, jeez she could shoot pool. Jealous now of Barbie's pool playing, Aggie looked for something more to drink. If she could get drunk enough she could fight somebody about something. She wasn't that drunk though. And who'd want to fight just 'cause someone else was shining up as a good pool player?

She just wanted him. She looked around and felt very alone.

Ronny, Chuckie and Aggie scraped together enough for a can of beer and the three of them made short work of it. Aggie moved slowly over to Johnny, stopping here and there, looking for somebody to bite for a drink. She was confident since everyone—well, almost everyone—knew that she was good for it. But it was too late and no-one had any money left. She sat next to Johnny. She felt like a chameleon, ready to be what he wanted her to be, moving to snare him, catch his eyes in hers, but he was looming large playing what he played, doing what he did, and reeling her in. He handed her his can of beer. Good sign, she thought. Imagined as the pub started to close, what might happen? She'd end up beside him somewhere, maybe sleeping with him. Drunk. The morning.

He turned around in his chair, looked at her square on.

'You better get that last train home eh? I'll walk you up the station.'

Johnny picked up her handbag and walked out without looking back at anybody. It was these little moves that impressed her. Had he watched a lot of hero movies? She didn't care. The air was cool and fresh outside. Hardly any cars or people, just Johnny and Aggie. He was still carrying her bag. She had to get the last train. Home. Where would he go? Where would he sleep? He could go back to the pub and maybe find someone to buy another carton and drink till dawn. Anything could happen.

He reached out and shook her hand.

She shook his hand and said thank you.

That was it then.

Certainly, it was just the beginning.

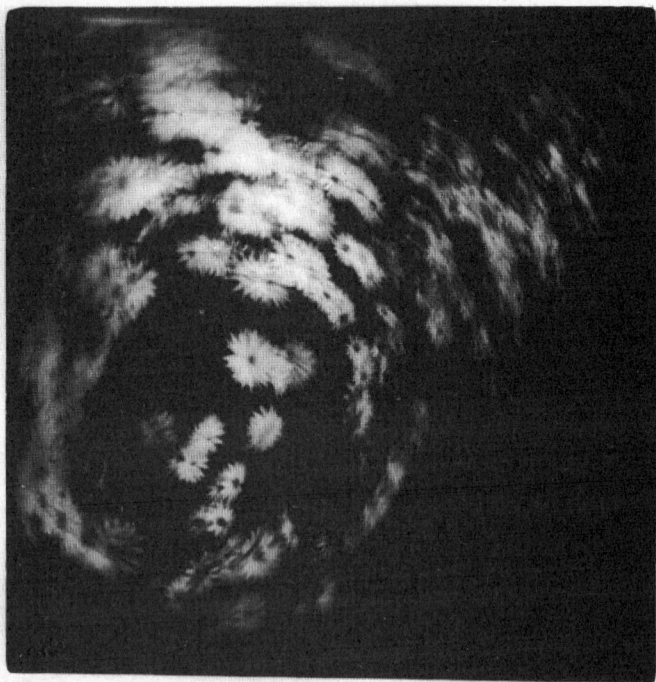

Rocco Fasano

TRESPASSING

Simon Colvey

I'm the guy who drove Damian Tiers there. We were all hanging out at this club, sinking beers out on the balcony when Damian rolled up. He'd come straight from the set of this student film he had been acting in and as he strode over to where we were all loudly standing he menacingly declared, 'Fuckin' Richard is dead meat.' Of course none of us took him seriously. A drawn-out moment of silence followed before someone finally said, 'What the fuck are you talking about?'

'I fuckin' know what's going on, that's what.' Damian glared back at us, his silvery eyes dancing with venom, as if we were all somehow to blame. 'I know the whole fuckin' story. All of it.' His voice was caged in a steely disgust that no-one particularly wanted to acknowledge. It was Friday night and our priorities hankered after our darting gazes. New Year's had come and gone, summer was addressing its molten peak, and everywhere a torpid abandon seemed to have prevailed amongst the swell of the 2 a.m. crowd.

'What story?' I said with icy abruptness.

His head snapped around and he looked at me like I was a complete stranger.

'How fuckin' Judy is cheating on me.'

I, like most others, already knew what Damian had obviously only recently learnt. For some reason victims are always the last to know even when they are the first to find out.

Damian went on a bit, about what a slut Judy was, how he was going to get Richard, other stuff. We all just stood around nodding, now and again vaguely sympathising or offering up a rueful condolence. I didn't really know Judy too well, or for that matter Damian. And I didn't really care. It was their business as far as I was concerned and I'm sure everyone else felt the same way.

As it turned out I was the lucky one who ended up running into Damian right toward the end, when the last shards of those who still remained were being herded into the foyer. By this stage he was off his head and it would be claimed later he had taken E and acid over the course of the evening. He spotted me there in the tight press of people and pushed his way over and when he reached me he jabbed his arm out and lunged like a fencer.

'Bravo,' I said. 'Very clever.'

Damian didn't say anything. He just gave off this almost maniacal laugh while repeating the action over and over. Apparently in the student film there had been a scene where two characters ended up having a sword fight. Or something like that. Many of the smaller details of that night have been either lost or permanently blunted. In the end I had to tell him to quit it and when he wouldn't I simply moved off and left him there. He followed me out onto the street and in the soupy gauze of dawn he asked if I could give him a lift around to Judy's place, since it was on my way. It never occurred to me in that moment just how foolish people can be.

Maybe I was simply being naive. I probably was. But at the time I swear I never anticipated what Damian had already instinctively fathomed. To this day I believe he knew what was going to happen. After all, the three of them together had scripted it. As for myself and the part I played, I was drunk, tired, indifferent. And who could have ever imagined just how far he would take it.

We didn't say much as I drove him there. No doubt he was rehearsing what he was going to do. I let him off and the last thing he said to me was thanks. See you around. I never saw him again.

Because as I continued on home he let himself in. Went into Judy's bedroom. And with a similar action to the one he had been practising on me, stabbed Richard.

Simone shifts and slings her arm across my chest. Her breath sighs and she softly murmurs something. Outside the low throaty moan of a cat issues petulantly as it slinks by. I lie there awake, for some reason unable to get back to sleep and lost in the fog of these thoughts.

I've never really understood just what propelled Damian to do what he did. But then I suppose I've never truly felt any great remarkable sentiment for anyone. Don't ask me why. It's not as if there haven't been a few close calls. But in the thrall of those early years I was always someone more intent on other things it seemed.

My studies. Going overseas and travelling. Then my
career. I suppose I just wasn't pinned down long enough.
Or it turned out in the end they weren't really the one.
I can't answer you why the lack of company didn't bother
me more than it maybe should have. It just didn't. And
then I met Simone.

Gently I roll onto my side and reach across for my
watch on the bedside table. Five in the morning. Simone
follows me in her sleep and as I lay my head back on
the pillow she cocoons herself around me, her hot skin
sending a rush of warmth into my own. We met at some
mutual friend's party several months ago and ever since
then we've developed into quite an item. Only the other
day, as I drove her back from work, she wondered aloud
if maybe we shouldn't move in together.

'We could see how it goes,' she offered brazenly in
order to mask her tentativeness. 'If you want to.'

I looked upward through the windscreen, saw spokes
of sunshine spearing through the leafy green canopy we
sped under, and I couldn't have felt lighter and happier.

Yet now, as I lie here, I am troubled and anxious and
full of doubt. I know I shouldn't be. And what's more,
harbouring such feelings isn't going to make any difference in the long run. I can only wait and see what
happens. Simone knows how I feel. And that's about as
much as I can expect.

'Okay then, well I'll ring you. Alright.' Simone stands
there in her padded pink dressing gown, in the doorway,
a warm affectionate smile creasing her face. I can't
understand how, but with every day she seems to become
prettier and prettier.

'Sure,' I go. 'That'd be great.' I give her the best
natural smile possible. 'Well. You know. I hope the dinner

goes well.' Of course I actually want it to be an unmitigated disaster.

'Thanks,' she says sweetly. 'I promise I'll call you tomorrow morning.'

'Okay.' I am all nonchalance and poise for her benefit. 'That'd be great.'

She steps forward and gives me a big hug then, and for a moment I feel as if a great weight has shifted off me and everything now lying ahead is safe. We share a long kiss before I finally struggle away and, clicking the gate shut, I turn to see her one more time. Dark hair out and falling to her shoulders. The smooth porcelain of her Eurasian features, the dark boyish eyebrows, the dainty nose, the plummy lips. I flick my hand in a truncated wave and uncrossing one arm she does the same back.

The morning shimmers with brightness and in the high blue enamel of the sky not one single cloud can be seen. It is indeed a glorious day and one that should not be spent brooding and wallowing in dark thoughts. I wish it was that easy. If Simone's ex, Tim, were some anonymous piece of her past then maybe I could stomach him voyaging out of nowhere to request one final date before he departed from her life entirely (this entailing him moving to Sydney to work for Mojo's as a creative director). The fact is though Tim has been a constant shadow draping our relationship ever since it began. He is forever ringing Simone, dropping in on her, sending old photos of them cuddled together on a back porch step (I found them in a letter I 'came across' one afternoon when I went snooping through her drawers while she was out.) I have gone around to her place to be greeted with her curled on the bed, sad and wanting to be held, because he had been around there earlier in the day. I even had to endure on a vacuous street corner, out the front of a 7-11 not so long ago, her proclamation that she still loved him. I have wanted to punch the guy out on numerous occasions for simply not having the decency to just butt out. Instead though I have remained a moderate, entrusting my faith in her, and hoping she feels the same way. Well, tonight I imagine I will find out just where we stand. Because I'm no fool. I know what Tim's up to. And in a funny way I don't really blame him. Since, if it came right down to it, I'd probably do the same thing.

I drive straight to work, forgoing my ritual coffee at the Victory, and as soon as I'm through the sliding doors I'm wishing I paid more heed to the DJ's tip, taken a sickie and gone to the beach. But I'm afraid the enormous amount of money I make must claim a portion of my soul.

Debra, a skinny waif who favours a rigueur of black attire, comes screaming over.

'I need film and proofs by this afternoon,' she announces like it's the end of the world otherwise.

I'm still really bleary from no sleep so all I reply is, 'Oh.'

Mind you, this isn't *any* client, and while I don't necessarily share Deb's tweedy urgency I am appreciative of deadlines. We're doing this new campaign to launch yet *another* fragrance on to the market and big bucks are involved. The client wants these huge banners created, which will be hung in shopping malls and on buildings throughout the country, but I'm afraid the design I have come up with so far still needs some attention. There goes my afternoon at the beach. As I stroll over to the coffee machine Deb hustles around me.

'We'll have to get a mock-up by lunchtime,' she tells me. 'If we do that we should be okay. I'll get Caroline on to it. If you get me your stuff by lunchtime. Then I can send it straight off.'

I simply offer a shrug and a 'whatever'.

'Well,' Deb continues. 'Is that okay?'

'Sure,' I go, a little too indifferently.

'I need it by lunchtime.'

'Fine.'

'Because if they don't get it . . .'

I'm not sure why but suddenly I am infused with rage. I stop in my tracks and pivot around to face Deb.

'Can you just shut up please,' I virtually spit into her face.

Deb's angular features instantly freeze and for a horribly extended pause she says nothing, leaving me feeling like a complete idiot, as I sense eyes claiming the scene.

'Fine,' Deb at last says in a blunt accusative voice. 'It's on your head.'

And with that she strides off.

The day moves arduously through its stages. Thank God I'm pretty busy for most of it. I don't even take lunch, preferring instead to shelter in the air-conditioned climes of the building and remain immersed in the tasks at hand. Come eight then and I'm knackered. That's when Rob, one of the junior art directors, appears beaming in the doorway of my office.

'You looked fucked mate,' he jovially points out. 'You up all last night rooting?'

'Very funny,' I say leaning back in my seat and looking out the window. Streaks of pink and red ripple down over the silhouetted tree tops and roofs and the first bright stars can be seen in the deepening blue high above.

'Some of us are going up the Eagle. You wanna come?'

It's been a long day and I really should just go home and get a good night's sleep, only it's the last place I want to be right now. All day I've been plagued by unfocused visions of Simone and Tim seated at a restaurant table holding hands. Canoodling. Going back to her place. I also keep experiencing a shocking hollowness that soars through the pit of my stomach at what seems to be hourly intervals. I'm not coping and don't I know it.

'Why not?' I say. 'Just give us five.'

Rob cracks a wide grin.

'You're on,' he says, cheery as all hell and with that he promptly departs.

The Eagle is its usual spectacle of slender bottle blondes, brown midriffs exposed, beefed-up blokes, affected greetings and ravenous gazes. Along with the constant brittle cacophony and the barely heard thud of music from somewhere, it's all a bit grim. I just want to go home, find Simone, curl up beside her and go to sleep. Fat chance.

Sure enough it doesn't take me too long before I'm a little bit under the weather. Maybe I have been a fool to let Simone go to that dinner. I could have perhaps been more resolute about my feelings, stated them with more guile and passion. But that's not what I want. Or at least it's not how I want to be.

I get another drink. Fade out of the conversation. Think about those early days and how simple they were. When I hear a voice interrupt and say, 'You look miserable.'

I turn and am pleasantly surprised. She is dark-skinned, very pretty with dainty features and long straight dark hair, and I must say, easy to take refuge in.

'Thanks,' I reply.

'Dog get run over?'

'I'm just really tired,' I reassure her. Then add, 'I've had heaps on.'

I lean back against the wall and offer her a smile. She steps away from her group of friends who cluster around one of the high set tables and joins me.

'Is that so,' she says playfully.

'Yeah, you know how it goes. It's that time of the year isn't it?'

'You need a holiday,' she says, sounding genuinely concerned.

I give a feeble shrug.

'Tell me about it.'

She comes even closer and I notice then she also has had a few.

'I want to go out,' she moans coquettishly.

'You *are* out,' is my brilliant reply.

'Somewhere more exciting. Like where you can dance.'

'What about your friends?'

She rolls her eyes and grins.

'They're boring.'

'Are they now?' I say.

I offer a toast. She clinks my glass and once more I receive another of her delicious smiles.

'What do you do?'

'Me?' I can't help grinning and suddenly I find myself looking straight into her sleepy black eyes. 'I'm an art director.'

'Another one.'

'I know.' I cast my gaze in a panorama through the place and as I do this I suddenly see him, emerging out of a knot of people and sidling over to the bar. My heart leaps into my mouth and all I can do is stare.

'You don't know Sebastian Riley, do you?' I hear her say.

'Sebastian Riley?' I repeat in a daze.

Of course in the waxy dimness I can't be entirely sure it really is him. Still. The wavy dark hair. The solid build. His open and neatly set features. I simply can't believe it.

'He's with Greys.' But I'm miles away. Thinking it's not inconceivable. He could be out by now. It's possible. 'Hello.'

'What?' I return my gaze to her. 'I'm sorry. Look. Um. It was nice meeting you.'

Her features melt into a perplexed disappointment.

'I'm sorry,' I hopelessly offer again. 'It's too complicated to explain.'

I feel so edgy, brittle and lost right then. I leave her with yet another abrupt 'sorry' and somewhat tepidly I ease my way through the bodies and elbows. Damian, or whoever, relaxes against the bar, leans on an elbow and scans for the attention of one of the blonde barmaids. I simply cannot take my eyes off him and as I grow closer my mind reels. It really is him. It really is.

Damian now pricks a bill scissored between two fingers into the air. I ease around the corner of some bull mastiff masquerading as a human and hesitate. Damian stands only a few feet away. One of the barmaids goes over to him and he leans forward so she can hear him. *Why am I doing this?* I think. I don't even want to see him again. I got so much flack from Richard's girlfriend when she found out I had driven Damian there. She went right off the handle at me one night at this party, claiming I should have known better. She's never forgiven me.

Then there's Judy, carrying the horror of that night around with her for the rest of her life. For what?

And then I'm there. Sliding next to Damian and resting my forearm gently down on the bar. Staging my next move. What I'm going to say. The barmaid returns carrying his drink. She places it in front of Damian and he pays. Nearby someone laughs and shouts, 'That's what they always say.' I swivel my head, look over my shoulder.

Out of the corner of his eye he notices and as he clutches the base of the glass he turns.

'Damian?'

He smiles broadly and I feel ashamed.

'I think you've got the wrong person, mate.'

Not long into our relationship Simone and I had been out attending a fashion show, and afterwards there was a 'hit and run' party at this club. Simone was tired and didn't want to go so she went home while I, asserting my independence, tagged along with some friends.

When we got there, I almost immediately wanted to leave. The place was wall-to-wall with the high couture beautiful set and that night I had no voyeuristic inclination. Yet at the same time neither did I wish to appear at Simone's bedside so shortly after leaving her. I was settling myself in then for the long haul, tailoring my conversation toward the banal, and generally doing my best to adapt to the forced gaiety (while all the time counting the minutes) when I suddenly saw something I liked.

She was sitting up at the bar, with some guy who had his back to me, and initially my only interest was physical. As she was wearing a very short skirt I was presented with an uninterrupted study of her long legs and as I spied on her I was disappointed to note the laughter and faint touches this guy managed to elicit from her. Nonetheless, my gaze kept instinctively returning to her, much to my bewilderment, and then, to top it all off, I began to experience a growing electricity of recognition. Curiosity got the better of me and I decided to wander past and take a closer look. I drifted by, all eyes, my memory then careering to the inevitable when I heard my name called. I looked over and was happily surprised to discover that the guy she was with was Tom, a vague industry friend who worked for a rival agency. He waved me over enthusiastically and when I joined them he promptly introduced me. She smiled and extended her slim hand.

'Hi,' she said as I took it. 'I'm Judy.'

Of course I was stunned and for a few long moments I just stood there, lost for words, as a coterie of singular moments gushed through my mind. A moment on a leafy summer street as she walked to work; her aloof seductiveness out on the balcony; the night we ended up slouched together in a couch at some party. Her soft dark eyes hovered knowingly over me as I held her hand.

'We've met before, haven't we?'

'Yes, we have,' I said, giving nothing away.

'You knew Damian?' She asked this without any malice or accusation.

'Not really,' I said, maintaining my cool. 'We were never friends. Just, you know.' I hurriedly searched for the right and least antagonising description. 'We just knew each other around. We were never close or anything.'

Judy's face showed no emotion and I had the distinct impression her comment was merely to serve the purpose of placing me more specifically. The lethargic strains of an acid jazz track filtered through the clamour of voices and tinny pockets of laughter as I waited for her response.

'Oh,' she said as if she were distracted. 'I used to see you around a lot though. Didn't I?'

I wanted to remind her about our brief indulgence on the couch but instead I merely played along.

'Sometimes.'

'Yes,' she mused to herself. 'Your face does look familiar.'

Tom interrupted us then and offered to buy me a drink. He left us there and Judy and me got talking about what she was doing now. She told me she was living up in Sydney these days and working as an actor. She proudly went on to tell me how she had just finished shooting a 'major' film which would be out sometime in the new year. In rather affected and pretentious tones I heard all about who had directed it, where it had been shot, the other lead actors I must know about and how she had played one of the main roles. In the ensuing several years she had seemingly developed into a highly self-absorbed individual who had no difficulty in crapping on endlessly about herself. As her manicured voice spieled out the details, the high and lows, the praises and acknowledgments she had reaped whilst on the set, my attention gradually began to glaze over.

Tom finally returned with my drink and I suppose I could have taken the opportunity then to leave them to it. I didn't though. Being perfectly honest I found Judy very attractive. Age certainly hadn't stolen her looks. Long straight blonde hair, she would remind you of one of those Californian beach types (all legs, no hips, with a sweet fresh face), and I'm afraid old flames were reignited. Added to this, knowing she was down from

Sydney, well I guess I wanted to play it right out, just to see.

So I hung around for a bit, had another drink yet generally, in the end, paid more attention to the time rather than Judy. My beautiful Simone awaited me, cosy and warm in the haven of her bed, and this thwarted any real desire on my behalf to become involved in the limited conversation dictated by Judy. Indeed, all nostalgic desire for her quickly evaporated in the face of her relentless egocentrism and in the end I couldn't get out of there fast enough.

Yet when I went to leave, offering the weak excuse of having to be on location early for a shoot, Judy declared she also needed her sleep. It turned out she was modelling in the fashion show for some designer she knew and she claimed she wanted to save herself for the final parade tomorrow night. Tom didn't seem too fussed when she asked me if her hotel was on my way. I myself was more puzzled about why she even bothered, since I had said virtually nothing to her and shown even less interest.

In the car we swept through the gentle warm night, the all but deserted late night streets swimming past like a dream in their hazy glow. Songs of the moment murmured from the radio as we temporarily gave ourselves up to the motion and the whoosh of wind through the open windows.

'It can be such a beautiful city,' Judy finally said in a dreamy voice.

'I suppose so,' I replied.

From somewhere not too far off the monotonous thump and boom of a car stereo peaked momentarily, then rapidly dwindled.

'You know he gets out soon,' she went on, as if she were really talking to herself.

'When?'

'Next month I think. On good behaviour. That's what I heard anyway.' She didn't sound very sure but I didn't press her. 'I don't want to be here.'

'No,' I feebly replied. 'Why would you?'

I glanced over at her. Her face was turned away from me, intent on the thick shadowed sidewalks we swept past.

'Do you ever think about that night?' she said softly.

The subject hadn't been broached all evening, although this was hardly surprising given the setting and Tom being there with us. Also I had hoped that maybe our previous loose connection in history would have assured no mention of the topic.

'Not really,' I said. 'Sometimes. But hardly ever now.'

'I think about it all the time.' Her tone was matter-of-fact. 'Not always. But a lot still.'

'I'm sorry,' I offered, not knowing really what to say. I could only imagine the horror of what she had witnessed that night. And even then it was only in some highly artificial manner since I'd had no experience of death, other than a grandmother passing away peacefully.

'It's okay,' she said haphazardly. 'I thought he was going to kill me too. But I suppose you don't hurt what's yours.' This last part was tinted with scorn.

'No, I guess not.' I wanted to reach across and touch her, but I couldn't.

'I was a silly girl then,' she mused half-heartedly.

'It wasn't your fault.'

'No, I suppose not.' She shifted in her seat slightly and smoothed the top of her thigh. 'But sometimes it doesn't really help.'

I stuck my bottom lip out, nodded and we spoke no more about it. Some cars coming the opposite way, their headlights dazzling across the windscreen, sliced past. I stared straight ahead and thought about Simone, asleep, expecting me at any moment. Judy here beside me. Why now? I wondered. Why not a couple of months earlier?

When we got to the hotel Judy hesitated before she got out.

'Do you want to come inside for a smoke?' she asked demurely.

I looked at her there in the soft sheen of the dash light, dark shadows clinging around the hollows of her cheeks, under the pockets of her eyes. I was reminded again of that night she and I ended up on the couch kissing. We were both drunk, there, willing to make the moment so much more. It never went beyond that. For some reason I didn't run into her again until months later and by that time she was seeing Damian. Everyone fancied her back then.

I smiled and said no.

My hand was resting on the gearstick and I felt her own hand slide on top of it then.

'You sure,' she said.

I kept my idiotic smile and tried to be as polite as I could. My answer was already prepared.

'Really, it's okay,' I said. 'I've got heaps on tomorrow.' A total lie. 'Thanks anyway.'

Judy's hand crimped around my own and exerted a wonderful faint pressure as she waited to see if I would change my mind. A fuzzy breeze angled through the street, grazing the branches of a tree on the corner, its lank leaves eddying slightly.

'Well,' she finally said. 'I might see you tomorrow night. At the show.'

'Sure,' I said.

'Just come backstage and ask for me.'

'Okay.'

'It was nice seeing you again.'

'Same here.'

Judy offered one final smile, an almost apologetic one it seemed, and a crease of vulnerability appeared to shade her features. A long moment passed and I wondered about all sorts of things. About loneliness. About how we try to fend it off all the time. How when it rains it pours.

'Night,' Judy finally whispered.

Her hand slipped off. The door clunked open and she got out.

I carefully unlatch the gate and cautiously stroll up the gravel path, in two minds. A more level-headed part of me knows I shouldn't even be here. This is ridiculous. *What are you doing?* a voice inside my head screams through the murkiness. You don't even trust her. But how can I when she never called?

I feel washed out, airy and around my eyes the skin feels puffy and drawn. I barely slept a wink last night (two in a row now) and I haven't even had anything to eat. I should just turn around, right this instant, and be done with it. But I can't. I have to know.

A couple of cars sear past, followed by the lumbering groan of a bus, before the early morning tranquillity settles in once more, bringing with it a crisp hush, broken only by the odd chirp of a bird.

Reaching the door I go to knock when I suddenly hesitate. What if Jennie, her housemate, answers? What do I do then? I glance behind me to see if the coast remains clear, then I take a quick peek through the spy-hole. The exaggeratedly curved panorama of an empty and gloomily lit hallway is all I am greeted with. No harsh glare emanates from the kitchen at the far end, nor do any pale blocks of light fall through the doorways of those rooms off the hallway. I stay like that for a bit longer, face pressed up against the door, but no signs of life disturb the scene. It would appear that if she is indeed home then she is still in bed. I do not even want to begin to consider the alternatives.

I step back and remain fixed to the spot. A tight knot twists itself in the centre of my chest and once again I consider just pissing off. I really don't want to do this. But coming this far, seeing what I've seen. Quite simply, I have to find out now. Like it or not.

Mustering courage I take the icy plunge and knock. Three brittle considered knocks. Then I wait. My thoughts at this stage are racing to all sorts of ludicrous tangents. She is in there with him, snuggled asleep. They're at his place fucking this very moment. He's not there. She's simply sleeping alone. I've just woken her up. What am I going to say? I strain to hear the muffled tread of footsteps approaching and prepare myself for the scratch and clunk of the lock as the door opens. Another set of cars whoosh past and from somewhere not too far off a dim voice shouts, 'I'll see you tonight.' Then a car door thumps shut and an engine gags into a loud vroom.

It appears no-one is home, including Jennie–how fortunate. I peer through the spy-hole again to make sure and as I'm doing this I give another knock. Still no-one appears. My previous fatigue by now has vanished, replaced instead with taut adrenalin. I know what I'm going to do next and this is the maddest part. What's done is done and my breaking her confidence will serve no good purpose here. Other than maybe seal my fate once and forever.

A jazzy thrill grips me as I unlock the door. I received this key not long into our relationship and ever since then I have remained eternally respectful, only ever using it to keep those midnight rendezvous and to place bunches of flowers without her knowing. I gently close the door behind me and just stand there for a few moments, ears intent, a huge gaping emptiness spreading through me as my heart pounds away. A cavernous silence remains outside, punctuated by the odd muffled breeze of a passing car. I creep down the hallway, my gaze scouring for evidence of deceit. A sock. A shoe. His jacket maybe hanging from one of the pegs just inside the doorway. I come up with nothing.

Her bedroom is the second room just before the loungeroom and when I reach it I tentatively crane my head around the partially open door. I don't know why but I'm still half expecting to find her there fast asleep. I'm disappointed though. All I see is an empty bed in one corner, the doona pulled back and an almost full glass of water on the bedside table. Pale sunlight dapples the room and over near the window a school of dust particles hover gently. I go over and sit on the bed, temporarily at a loss about what to do now. She is not here and in some respects this can be considered strange, although another part of me is relieved to know that it does appear she spent the night here. I reach over and pick up the clock radio on the bedside table, checking to see what time the alarm was set for. Six-thirty. A hollow dread collapses through me. This I know to be way too early.

Cradling the clock radio in my lap I fiercely debate the now apparent distinct possibility that he has been

here. This time was set for him. For his work. Or maybe
he was catching that flight to Sydney. Maybe they
decided to indulge in one final romantic breakfast somewhere. In all this I simply cannot figure why she would
get up so early today. Usually she's never up before ten.
It just doesn't make sense.

The room aches around me and I feel foreign to
everything I have grown so accustomed to. Her bed. The
articles of furniture. The simple presence and sense, the
light, the vague mandarin odour, the scraps of clothing
usually littered across the floor. I cannot help finding
Damian's sullen features in this moment, shadow and
light slipping across them as I drive him there. An intense
moody quiet commands from him as he steadily watches
straight ahead. I can even remember the song that was
playing on the tape. One by REM.

That night I dropped Judy home I came straight here
afterwards and as I let myself in I couldn't help wondering if I hadn't made a mistake. Since it was entirely up
to me whether I turned up or not, though as Simone and
I shared a farewell kiss I could tell she wanted me to
surprise her. And undressing in the darkness I thought
about where I could have been right then and if it would
have ever mattered. But when I climbed into bed and
Simone immediately embraced me, I knew better. I snuggled into her and kissed her lightly.

'You met someone, didn't you?' she murmured.

For a moment I thought about what I should say, then
told her yes.

'I knew you had.'

'Really?' I asked, masking my astonishment at her
intuitive powers.

'Uh-huh.' Her hand smoothed across my belly. 'I
knew you didn't really want to go to that party.'

'No,' I replied.

'It doesn't matter,' she crooned.

I rolled onto my side and pushed myself into her. I thought about telling her Judy was the girl I met and everything that happened. But that seemed too complicated.

'She was boring and I kept on thinking about you here,' was all I told her instead.

That was enough for Simone. Her hand reached further down and I pulled her into me.

Suddenly the reasons for my being here seem very elusive. I reach back across to replace the clock radio, less burdened now, though still intrigued as to my darling's whereabouts. I'm sure there is a reasonable enough explanation and deeper down I somehow know nothing untoward has taken place. I stand and survey the room one more time. From the kitchen I hear the fridge click and come on, it's deep purr seeping through the rooms. I'm an arsehole and don't I know it. Time to go. It briefly occurs to me I could leave a note but I think better of it. Best to leave things as they are and just see what happens. Nothing necessarily has been lost or gained. Though then again, who's to say otherwise?

I guess in time I'll find out.

Simone returns from the kitchen with the tea.

'Your lordship,' she quips as she sets down my cup on the coffee table on which I have my feet propped.

'Where's my fuckin' dinner?' I joke back.

I receive a playful thump on the shoulder for this comment before she slouches down into the couch.

'Do we really have to watch this?' she says as she snuggles against me.

'Darling.' My tone is all smug haughtiness. 'It's the World Series.'

'I hate cricket,' she sighs.

Her head tips and rests against my shoulder.

'But the Australians are winning, honey.'

No reply comes and instead the gentle reflective murmur of the commentary rises up and solidifies. Her hand slinks between my legs, burying itself near my crotch. I am a lucky man today, I think. As it turned out Simone had to do a breakfast shift and that is why the alarm was set so early. Of course I didn't find this out until that evening when I finally got through to her. I tried all day without any success, left one message at the hotel, two on her answering machine. And then when I was finally home I had to deal with her line being engaged. You can imagine how I felt. She ended up filling in for a girl and doing a lunch as well. She said she never got my message at the hotel. Was too tired when she got home to immediately return my call. Then her mother rang.

How did I ever allow myself to fall into that trap? She has told me in vague terms what happened with Tim. How he proposed. Invited her up to live in Sydney. She has provided scant other details and in a way I don't care to know them. Her presence here, now, is her decision and this is good enough for me.

The afternoon peels lazily away. The half-drunk tea grows cold and two blocks of sunlight fall across the floor. Outside a dog starts yapping away, then abruptly stops. Voices on the street mumble past the window. Cars hiss by. A neighbour's door wheezes open and bangs shut. Laughter. Her warm breath against the nape of my neck. Pulling her closer, she nibbles my ear lobe as I reach under her blouse. Feel her breast. Her lips. Applause crackling from the television.

Three loud knocks suddenly issue down the hallway. Simone goes rigid and pulls away from me slightly.

'Forget it,' I whisper.

The lustrous glaze to her eyes vanishes and she twists her head in the direction of the door. I go to kiss her, rekindle our momentum, but she's having none of it.

'No,' she tells me succinctly. 'I want to see who it is.'

I relax back into the couch. She stands, tucks herself in, feathers her hair, and gives me a 'wait-till-later smile'.

'As long as it's not the Mormons,' I call after her.

'What?' I hear her yell back.

'Nothing,' I mutter.

I return to watching the cricket, settle myself. Hear the door open and the echo of the street. Then suddenly *his* voice, bewildered and hysterical.

'See. See. See what you've done to me?' he screams. 'This is what you've done.'

I'm up in a flash and flying down the hallway. Her voice struggles to intrude as he continues screaming at her.

'You did this to me. YOU DID THIS.'

'Tim. Oh my god,' I hear her saying. 'Jesus. Come here.'

'You bitch. See. Do you see now?'

'Tim.'

I'm there. Heart racing. Their voices, confused, loud, boom around the porch vestibule. Simone, her back to me, reaches a hand up to her face. I come up beside her, grab her around the shoulder and see him then, there. His screwed up features barely take me in as he holds the arm out in front. Thick trails of blood slide all over the flesh, congeal at his finger tips and splatter over the concrete. What appears to be a huge gash runs down the inside while other smaller cuts are scattered around it.

'Tim please,' Simone implores, her hand now gripping her cheek.

'You did this,' he shrieks. The arm hovers there for another long second. 'Do you see now,' he says, voice breaking.

The tears he has kept back arrive then and as they stream down his cheeks he pivots and flees.

'Tim,' Simone cries feebly after him.

He doesn't turn around. He barges out the gate and jumps into a waiting red-coloured car. It indicates, pulls out, and speeds off.

Back inside Simone is a shell of pensive brooding. I try my best to console her but it has little effect. She sits on the couch, a stony facade pondering all the things I'd like her to tell me. I don't intrude. I remain at a respectful distance, in a chair diagonally opposite her, and wait.

'I have to go to the hospital,' she finally says. 'See if he's there anyway. The Alfred.' She looks at me with an inquiring expression.

'Probably,' I offer. 'It's the closest.'

She returns her gaze to the television. An umpire traces the shape of a square with his two index fingers as he asks for a photo.

'I'll drive you there.'

'No,' she says. 'I'll be alright. You wait here.'

She knows how much this last part means to me.

'You sure?'

She nods.

'Whose car was that he got into anyway?' I ask as she stands up to go.

'His new girlfriend's.'

'You're kidding.' I'm stunned. 'He gets his new girlfriend to drive him around here.'

Simone looks over at me like she didn't catch what I just said. She doesn't say anything and I keep my mouth shut. Reluctantly I rise. On the bloody top step we share a hug and I tell her I'll be here. Call me if she wants to. I hope he's okay. We kiss and she brushes her hand against my cheek.

'Thanks,' she says.

'It's alright,' I tell her, trying my best to be as diplomatic as possible.

Her hand slips away and she turns. I go to say something but nothing comes out. Instead I can only mutely watch her walk down the path and when she reaches the front gate I half expect her to turn and wave. She doesn't.

Long shadows slip across the small garden and here and there warm patches of gold sunshine collect. A perfect stillness is here now, broken by not one sound. Insects hover around the flowers. A veil of pollen spreads upward. An aeroplane high above silently glides across the sky. Who's to say how I'm going to act when I find out she has left me? I can't even begin to imagine. I take her presence for granted these days and I can't even remember any more what it was like without her.

Last night I woke up with such a start. Everything felt so empty and as I lay there in the darkness I felt sorry. For what I'm not exactly sure. And after a while I could hear the gentle sigh of Simone's breathing and the steady ticking of the clock and these sounds reassured me. So that I closed my eyes and returned to sleep.

In the aeroplane its passengers look down and see the sprawl of tiny roof tops, the swimming pools and the network of roads. They see Simone driving to the hospital, confused and at a loss. But they don't know this. The back of my neck tingles. I feel the softness in the air. Smell lilac.

GRACE

Kirsten Tranter

It's late in the day and Glebe Point Road is quietening down from its usual Saturday hum. I'm sitting on a latte, picking free postcards from the rack, filling each one with more or less the same news to people in Melbourne, Perth, Berlin, Bondi. The most important news is that the weather is gradually getting cooler. This is something I'm sad about. The late afternoon slides in, slow and cheerful. I'm about to start on another card when a surprise walks into the dim cafe.

My guts register a shock and once again I resent the pathetic interior of the body with its unwilled responses. While he walks towards me I click into a kind of steely coolness.

'Hi Peter.' With the light behind him he is a tall, smudgy angel.

'Hello, Adelaide.' He steps down into the automatic hug before I have a chance to breathe. His lips dive in for a kiss, always on the lips. I'm not quick enough to turn my cheek.

He pulls out a chair and eases into it. Easiness. Edgy and ungracious, I started to be suspicious long ago of this quality of his, apparent in the face of even the greatest adversity.

'Is there one here for me?' He picks up my postcards, smiling.

'No, actually.' It has been roughly a month since our last sad attempt at a conversation over the phone. By the time Peter left for Melbourne to take up his scholarship late last year, things were pretty ugly between us. Fallout from previous mangled relationships; older, more mysterious and entrenched forms of hostility and betrayal; any number of monsters started to eat us up. I didn't expect to see him again for a while.

'What are you doing in Sydney?' I ask him. His hair looks like it's growing out from being shaved, a brown halo of fuzz around his head. I experience an unsettling desire to stroke his scalp, which I restrain.

'Having a break, a visit. Catching up with people. How have you been?'

Something is melting. 'Okay. You know. Taking it easy.'

'What are you up to for the weekend?' His eyes are the grey of arriving clouds.

'I've got nothing planned,' I say. 'What about you?'

'I have the car. We could go somewhere.'

I pocket my postcards and the anthology of stories about bad sex I just bought second-hand. Something has been decided. 'Let's go.'

He still has the old brown Holden. The hopeless seventies style of the car is comforting. We sit together in the front seats. The blinker of danger settles into a low hum. Whatever happens now is part of a long stretch of unreasonableness that winds out to the horizon, long as the road.

Peter puts the key in the ignition but doesn't turn it. He pauses for a moment, then turns, and puts his hand against my neck, thumb pressing into my jaw just lightly. I'm trying for a look of tranquillity but it's not happening. There is an urgency between us when our eyes meet, and a note of panic sounds. I'm starting to feel confused about what I'm doing here, in a car with a boy I haven't seen for several months, who now looks like he wants to devour me.

'This is terrible,' he says. 'I really want you.' It feels inexorable, although it's not. I kiss him. His mouth is deep and wet. Our bodies strain.

'Let's go to the mountains,' I say.

Peter shrugs, leans away, turns the key. 'Okay.' The Holden lurches onto the road.

Once we hit the jammed strip of Parramatta Road out west, I become unreasonably happy. At Food Plus we buy coke, cigarettes and chips for the ride. Back on the road I fiddle with the radio. Another song about hetero-sexual tragedy. It'll do. The music fades in like a soundtrack.

'The mountains. D'you want to stay up there the night?' Peter asks, fingers drumming absently on the dash. Of course I do.

'We can stay at a pub.'

'Oh yeah. A pub. Cool.' Peter is smiling. He rarely shows his teeth. Before he left, this was a plan we had together, to get away for a weekend and stay at a pub somewhere in the country. Replenish, away from the city. I imagined an old wooden hotel with wide, generous verandahs, set on a dry plane. With very cold beer, and a square room with a dark wooden wardrobe and bed. In a new space we would be beautiful together. The image fused in my mind like an old sepia photograph. Of course, we didn't get around to it. Inevitably on weekends we would end up at a pub somewhere in the inner city, drinking too much, and spend tense days at each other's small flats in Newtown, arguing or fucking to avoid whatever it was that put the fear into us.

At the first town we come to in the lower mountains the only pub on offer sports hideous fluorescent signs promising shows, dancing girls, and topless barmaids. We cruise by. Peter hmms. I'm repulsed and curious. 'If I was a boy, I'd probably go to places like that,' I admit. 'Occasionally. Very secretively, so no-one would know. To check it out. It fascinates me. Like tacky porn shops.'

'Yeah, you would,' Peter responds. A man could fade into the background in a place like that. Peter is silent regarding his own experience, if any, of such places. He says, 'Disgraceful.' I like the way he says it. Mouth curving at the corner, he takes the last drag on his cigarette, and flicks it away. His elbow returns to resting just out the window.

We decide to stop for some food. My head's dizzy with caffeine, no lunch, and the brittle lust that has settled in for the ride. Over pizza the conversation is delicate. Topics to be avoided include his thesis, my writing, and what precisely we are headed for here. My apprehension sticks. Something is lurking, deeper than the return of any attachment that may have existed for either of us.

I'm remembering the tortured last weeks before Peter left for Melbourne. There was a brutality about it. All my best jewellery broke. The terrible bushfires began. These events appeared as a sign that it was time to make some major repairs.

His face tells me nothing about how he's feeling. This is how it always was. Trying to read him is an exhausting exercise. We are both by now in serious need of some alcohol. His hands are restless, loose. He grins. 'Shall we hit the road?'

The highway pans out gracefully towards the approaching sunset. Low in the sky the clouds are orange, burning. A kind of bleakness settles on me which is not unpleasant. Safety signs along the way ask us questions: How fast are you going? Driving at a solid speed, the car hugs the bends in the winding road. The way Peter's bones collect at the wrist is hypnotic. I stare at his hands on the wheel and listen to him shyly say that he missed me, '. . . kind of, in some ways,' he says, his head tilting. I know what he means. There were things about him, about being around him, that I didn't miss at all. Now I'm remembering good things, and seeing new things: a more centred look around the eyes; a thinner, browner face.

There's some light lingering when we get to Katoomba, bourgeois haven of the Blue Mountains. The cheaper, more picturesque pub is full for the night. We pull up to the Grahame, a square, puce-coloured establishment. It has a bar, football on the telly on Friday nights, and double rooms for forty dollars.

'This looks like the one,' I announce. The Holden pulls up outside and we head over to check in.

Inside the carpets exude a faint, familiar smell of beer and old vomit. We wait at the pine veneer counter inside the door for a person of authority to appear. The bar in the next room doesn't appear too busy. After what seems like a long while, the man in charge arrives sure enough, laid back, balding and rotund. Peter slips easily into mateship mode, nods the head, signs the book, hands over the cash. Room thirteen, second floor, bathrooms down the end of the corridor. Okay. The counter man slides over a smooth, cold key.

I walk to the stairs with Peter, past the entrance to the dead second bar where a banner advertises 'DISCO: TONITE! (SAT)'. Peter nudges me. 'Ragin'.' For sure. The stairs are wide and worn, and smell oddly like baked dinner. My legs feel suddenly leaden. It must be the drive. Peter takes my hand and pulls me along. The stretch along my arm feels goods. The wallpaper is everything I could have asked for, textured yellow felt on crusty beige, slightly peeling but not mouldy. Just seedy enough to make my skin tingle. I know we have arrived at the place we were headed for.

The door to room thirteen opens off a long corridor onto a small room. Square, yes, but not exactly generous. There's no sink, a single wooden chair, a bed covered in a violent pink chenille spread, and an elegant pine dresser topped with a large lace doily. It's not the room in the pub in my young imagination, but it's not bad either. The pink walls and tired carpet emit a soft shine of decadent possibility. Four steps take me from the door to the narrow window. Pulling aside the scrappy lace curtains I take in the view: car park and highway. The distant mountain is a burning ridge in the last glow of light.

'It's not exactly a vista.' Peter motions to the window's pathetic view.

'We can go out looking for vistas tomorrow if we want.' The word *we* sits weirdly in my mouth.

GRACE

Peter's giving me that look of intent, the one that frames a question not quite articulated. I want him to lie down on the bed like an offering. I consider explaining this desire to him, but a kind of emptiness begins to fill me. I'm nervous that he would do it, nervous thinking about how it would happen. His shoulder bones look lovely through his faded T-shirt but the thought of a beer is more appealing for the moment. I have a suspicion that I'll feel better about this whole thing when I'm drunk enough to be convincingly not responsible for my actions.

'Is it time for a drink?' I ask.

He replies, 'Yes.' For a moment his indifference infuriates me, then it passes. We leave the room and the door clicks shut behind us.

Down in the bar we settle at a table with uncomfortable stools. The Grahame is evidently not home to Katoomba's burgeoning young middle class: almost every person boasts a flanny or polyester stripes. All right. The place is not exactly crowded. From what I can see, the disco isn't going off tonight. Although the small dance floor is lit up with red gel, there's no-one on it. A few sad plastic chairs are scattered around the edges. Peter is rejoicing at the prospect of heavy drinking at a pub unencumbered by the need to drive at the end of the night. It's better than being in your own loungeroom: no scene of destruction to deal with in the morning, and the beer is on tap.

We share gossip about our mutual friends: what they're doing, who they are sleeping with, who's got a job and who hasn't, what parts of the world they are travelling, which band has broken up, whose car got stolen. And talk about Melbourne, city of flat streets, fashion sense and early closing. Since Peter has been away I have vengefully convinced myself that he is lonely and isolated down there, but it seems that I've been wrong. I'm searching for the hole I've left in his life. If it exists, it's not apparent now. He has already moved house three or four times in the few months he has been there. I have known him to be flighty. But right this minute, on the third round of beers, he is as grounded as our table which is inelegantly bolted to the floor. It sounds as though he's probably bored in Melbourne, but I could be wrong.

The evening rolls on, becoming relaxed. Tonight I am blessed: my erratic pool skills come good and I win a game with Peter against the locals. The two men are surprised at my hard handshake at the end of the game. We lose a small amount of money on the card machine. In Melbourne they have only just been legalised and are still a novelty in pubs, so Peter is keen to gamble. The logic of the game continues to defy me.

Over the next couple of hours I begin to like the place intensely: I like the bleeping card machines, I like the faded psychedelic carpet, I like the worn yellow tiles in the toilets with their long, ancient chains. Even the framed posters of semi-naked women draped over red sports cars don't seem so offensive. The ashtray on our table fills and begins to smell ugly. Peter's broad hand on my knee feels like a perfect weight. His eyes are getting strangely brighter. It's time to get down to business. His voice comes down like a muted bell. 'Take me upstairs to bed.' I'm still looking for the wisdom in this demand, this particular arrangement of ourselves, but I'm not arguing.

On our way out I notice a couple slow-dancing on the disco floor to a rock ballad. Her high white shoes rest beside her on the ground. They lean together in a

kind of slump, as though their falling bodies are support-
ing each other in a tenuous equilibrium.

Back in the room I feel like I'm wrestling, fighting,
when our bodies come together. In the dresser's mirror
we are one messy shadow. I wrench off his shirt, feel a
tender sorriness I can't see the details of his closely
freckled skin in the dark. There is passion there, somewhere beneath the surface. I seek it out like a jewel. His
intake of breath when my hands pull back his head to
expose his neck sends a weird rush through me. It's a
tingling sense of power. In a vaguely nauseating moment
I get a glimpse of the thing it is I'm after: to wreck his
suave indifference. To force him to a place of stupid
desire and vulnerability. To make him lose the plot. What
for? There's no time to analyse the situation: all I want
now is to swallow him whole. The worn tattoo on his
shoulder is a dark flash of rose as his arms reach around
to lift off my shirt. He says my name. I watch his body
bending.

He leans into me hard like panic. There is a grasping
neediness in his hands, the way they pull at me as if to
detach the flesh from my bones. All of a sudden a crazy
urge arrives in me: a desire to comfort him, shadowed
by a creeping need to cause injury. I cradle his bony face.
Beautiful. His head rises, follows my stroke like a kitten.
I wonder how his back would fall, pushed down onto the
bed. The weird violence of it unsettles me. There's only
one thing left to do. Remove the rest of his clothes, press
open his eyes and begin.

When I'm lying stretched out, exhausted, over Peter's
lean body, the comfort I feel surprises me. Then I remember the bushfires and a small anxiety sets in. We are
surrounded by quietness; the occasional car drives past

on the highway. Someone in a nearby rooms starts singing what sounds like Frank Sinatra. I'm about to consider
a question to him when he reaches for my coiling hair.
His mouth hits my neck. My breath collapses. Whatever
he's murmuring into my collarbone sounds fine for the
moment.

In the morning the sunlight seeping through the window
seems very bright. My head spins for a moment with the
unfamiliarity of the place: for a second I don't know
where I am. The feeling peels reluctantly away as my
legs stretch out against the thin sheets. Katoomba. Hang-
over. Ashtray mouth. I'd give anything for a glass of
water. Beside me Peter looks crumpled and perfect in
sleep.

Some more decisions have to be made. About direction, for what happens today. Peter's eyes open suddenly
and look clearly into my own. Awake he is bloodshot and
slightly fragile. He rolls and yawns and stretches lazily.
Relaxed. 'Good morning,' he says. 'Do you want to go
out for breakfast?' So civilised. Yes. Hot coffee and food.
Toast. With Vegemite, is what I'd like. Peter rolls on top
of me, warm breath on my skin. I start to crave the taste
of his mouth, smoky and stale and intimate. Our teeth
crash when we kiss. It's just beginning to get interesting
when he whispers 'fuck' into my shoulder and picks up
my watch from the floor beside the bed. 'We have to be
out of here by ten.' Fifteen minutes. We both squint
slightly for a second, wondering if it's enough time, but
the moment is broken. I don't want to let go of his bony
spine, but it has to be done.

Through the window the glimpse of bush is a million
shades of green, deep and infinitely detailed. We both
search for underwear and pull on clothes. The small room

with its grotty edges is a pleasantly sealed space, unde-
manding. Sitting on the sagging bed, pale in the mirror,
my face looks back at me. Seven minutes to go before
the accounted-for time finishes. My blood wants coffee
but I don't want to walk through the door into the cold
corridor. Peter comes and kneels before me like a sup-
plication, head close on my knee. I stroke his head
absently.

He says blandly, 'It feels good to be with you.' I
listen for the trailing off in his sentence, towards a 'but',
but it's not there.

It's true. For now, in the closely bordered space of
the Katoomba pub. I'm more interested in what will
happen once we finish breakfast and begin the inevitable
seedy drive towards whatever destination is decided
upon.

I lift his chin gently. 'Yes. This has been fun. And
you're going back to Melbourne.' It's a flat statement.

He shrugs, looks at the ceiling. 'I don't know, Adelaide. We were so fucked up before I left Sydney, but
now, it seems like we're getting on really well.' His eyes
narrow, focus on me. 'I didn't know what would happen
when I came up. I don't know if I want to stay in
Melbourne, it's not working out to be that great. I'm
thinking of coming back to Sydney.' He starts to push
his fingers through my hair. 'What do you think?'

It could happen, I think. I can imagine it. I'm scared
at how much I want it, however much trouble I seem to
have with happy endings. A chance to redeem our dodgy
past and unseemly horizons. And this is what it's all
about, I think: a desire for redemption through one
another, a misplaced drama of romance and salvation.
This is what forces the intensity, turns the stomach, edges

the bones with spite and adoration. I want to save him from himself. And to be thus accorded grace.

It is a seductive offer, and he remains eminently beautiful in the light of day. 'Yes, please,' I say to him, and offer him my house, my time, my affections and my body. He pulls me up to stand, hands around my hungry waist.

'All right then. Let's go.' The doorway has lost its sense of apprehension. Down the stairs, past the lobby's pine interior, out on the street the air is thin and crisp. We set off towards the main strip of Katoomba in search of breakfast. The day opens like the slick road after rain.

NIGHT ON GORE STREET

Richard King

It actually *was* a dark and stormy night.

I was home alone, the light from my room the sole star of illumination in an otherwise cold and brooding street. The wind blew through the branches, causing them to sweep and scratch against the glass in a way that I still wasn't used to, and which was still eerie and discomforting. The house was silent. A silence occasionally disturbed by the refrigerator junking and then purring into motion, the steady and heavy tick of the clock, the floorboards creaking restlessly. I was reading a book, the fire glowing warmly, a mug of Horlicks sitting unsteadily on five or six other books on the table beside my bed when suddenly, suddenly and with a growl, Oscar my dog, pricks up his ears, sniffs the air, shifts nervously and then leaps down from the bed.

Oscar has been my dog for two years, has followed me from share house in the inner city to share house, and does not prick up his ears without good cause. He is not a frivolous ear-pricker. I set my book down, listen with my inferior human ears for the noise that alerted him to danger, arm myself with the steering wheel lock I keep beside the bed, and then slowly and silently follow him up the hallway into the unmapped dangers of the house.

Look out. Be careful. My heart is beating like a time bomb with a particularly deep and resonant tick. More a thuddish beat really.

It's at about the point where I reach the kitchen that I register that I'm a 28-year-old, university educated man following around a 16-inch dog to see what might be an interesting thing to do on a Saturday night. And that's a fairly confronting realisation. Too many drugs. Too much alcohol. Not that Oscar is a poor activities coordinator. When I catch up to him in the back yard we happily bark at a fallen flower pot for six or seven minutes but I can't completely suppress the feeling that this is not what I should be doing with my Saturday night. That God and my parents and my house tutor might have envisaged bigger things for me than following around a puppy dog to find out what's fun.

This is not what fun is.
I ditch the quiet night spent at home reading and hanging around with a dog and ring some friends to gee up a night out.

This is what fun is.

Pub # 01.

— Which is kind of why we have to stop buying so much hardcore pornography.
— I completely beg your pardon.
— It's not politically correct.
— Politically correct?
— It's not sensitive to feminism.

It's an hour later and I'm sitting with my friends Sam and Jules down at the pub. My 'Alert!! Alert!!' sensors should have activated the moment I rang them and found that they did not have previous commitments on this Saturday night but as is the case with these situations, it is often hard to identify the precise moment when these evenings go sour. I said 'Are you up for a drink?' and then they said 'Sure. What time?' and I said 'About ten-ish,' and never at any point did anyone identify the moment when someone should have said, 'Hell. Maybe we should just leave it.'

Maybe we should have consulted Oscar. Oscar would have said 'ruff ruff' but I suspect would have intended 'No. It's late. Let's just write this night off. Go to bed.'

Instead, I find myself at the pub, listening to this:

— It's not politically correct. (Jules)
— Politically correct? (Sam)
— It's not sensitive to feminism.
— How on earth does feminism come into this? What

conceivable connection can you make between
hardcore pornography and issues of feminism?

— Because pornography degrades women. It presents
them as sexual objects, it sends messages that women
are tramps and sluts and whores, when publicly displayed it insults and disturbs women, and it
perpetuates a misogynist and anti-female society.

— Oh. I see.

Says Sam, and he pauses, considering this intently. After
a few moments (three), he says:

— Well. Bummer. That's the trade-off I guess. If that's
what society's got to wear to ensure the survival of
what is a very fine product, then that's just what
we're going to have to do.

— It isn't the trade-off. We have to get rid of hardcore
pornography. I've joined this group called Men
against Misogyny and part of our agenda is to see
the destruction of the hardcore pornography industry.

— What a dreadful group.

Says Sam and continues:

— What a bunch of fifth columnists. I'm very very anti
that club. In fact I would like to join the exactly
diametrically opposed club. Who are your biggest
enemies?

— You already are a member of that club.

Says Julian venomously.

— I wasn't aware. How did I join up?

— You join that club every time you buy hardcore pornography. That's your membership card.
— Well I didn't even know I was in the club. But I would have joined anyway. What a wonderful publicity idea. Join our club and you will get hardcore pornography. I wonder if there's any other clubs because I'd join them too. Maybe there's the odd stamp-collecting club or maybe our mother's golf club, *'Beryl . . . welcome to the club. Here's your T-shirt, your membership certificate and here's a bumper, ripper hardcore pornographic magazine called . . . well I don't really want to say what it's called. Well . . . you all see for yourself girls.'* Maybe that's what happens.

(These are my friends!! Help me.)

— No. I think they get badges. (Me)
— Oh. Well Mum should sound them out. She could give them to me.
— Ha ha Sam. You're just a pervert.
— Yep that's me. I like liking at photos of naked women. I'm the Sicko. Lock me up.
— Get fucked.
— God you're a loser. You've been a loser for twenty-four years and you're a loser now. Pussy-whipped by Kerri and a loser.

At this point Jules punches Sam and Sam punches me (I have no idea. I'd hardly said a thing.)
So the three of us get punched in the head (I don't punch anyone. A bouncer punches Jules.)
We get kicked out (quite correctly) and standing outside

181

in the chill night air, laugh, decide that was fun, and go to another pub.

Pub # 02.

— Anyone?
— Yeah I'm up.
— Same again.
— I'm in.

I kind of like these Saturday nights out with Sam and Julian. It's not as if we achieve anything (Well we do. We get drunk.) and it's not as if we momentarily relieve the depressing and disastrous circumstance that is our lives (Well we do. We get drunk.) and it's not even as if we momentarily fulfil our parents' expectations and manifest the potential we displayed in 1983 (Well we do. We get drunk.) It's more that, for a few brief shining moments, we're completely contented. We're completely where we should be and are. We're fully realised.

Though Oscar would probably dispute that.
What the fuck does Oscar know?
Uppity little canine shit.

Firstly picture me, standing at the bar, my left leg up on the bar, and moving it up and down to a tune that remains elusively about six beats ahead of me. Not the 'bar' bar. The bar that runs along the base of bars (which has a purpose I'm sure which I just can't identify unless of course it's to give drunk maggots something to put their left leg on while they fail to keep time with the music). I'm waiting for the manifestation of three drinks which I have wisely ordered when I am elbowed in the ribs in a way that isn't so much a 'Oops mate I'm sorry. You know what with the place being so crowded and all' elbow-in-the-ribs but more a 'You're that fucking cunt Eric Hardy you fucking cunt' elbow-in-the-ribs.

And I'm not just being paranoid.

I look around from the bar-attendant for the benefactor of this gift of male aggression and identify the person as the ex-boyfriend of an ex-girlfriend. (You just don't want to know what went on between the three of us but take it as said, I was completely in the right on all issues and on all occasions and at all times.) As this little aggro fuckin . . . as the person in question does not so much as deserve to feast on the excrement . . . is a man of mixed qualities . . . I don't even acknowledge him, but rather, in a way that Billy Idol has got down pat and that Elvis was pretty good at, do this half-lipped sneer and look back to the bar attendant only to have cock-sucker ex-boyfriend (see above) croon in my ear.

— How are you cunt? I guess you never knew but, the whole time you were going out with Jill, I was fucking her the whole time too.

Pause. Regroup, rebuild. Take it in your stride and hit back hard.

— Is that the case? Well I guess that means you're pretty much due for the same shit news I got from my doctor three weeks ago. Welcome to the death club.

And I take the drinks back to the table.

— Did you see that?

I ask Sam and Jules.

— What?
— I just saw fuck-brain at the bar. Can you see him?
— Yeah . . .
— How does he look?
— He looks white. He looks like death. What did you say?
— I discreetly suggested that he might be H.I.V. positive. He really looks scared?
— Terrified.
— Taken aback?
— And some.
— I do not need that little cunt in my life. Jules . . . ?
— Yeah?
— Do we know that woman over there? Don't look now but . . . look.

Jules looks behind him and over to the left at one of the two women I suspect I've met somewhere at sometime.

— Yeah. That's Julie.
— Julie?
— We went to her party about a month ago. Don took us.
— And I went?
— You remember. The night we tipped the taxi-driver more for taking five of us than it would have cost to hire another cab.

— How dumb.

— How fucked. The party was out in North Fitzroy.

— And . . . ?

— I don't know . . . it was just a party. We got spastic. You finished up leaving with Kate.

— Is she our friend?

— I don't know. You and Sean talked to her for a while. It was the night you got punched by the guy you used to go to school with.

— Oh I remember. I remember the party. Can't remember talking to anyone though. Did she like me?

— Fucked if I know. Doubt it. Unlikely.

— You can't remember whether I fucked up at all?

— How do you mean fucked up?

— Just 'generic, drunk, sleaze Eric Hardy' kind of fucked up.

— I can't recall.

— I've got this feeling I might have. I might go and say hello.

— Cool. I'll keep your seat.

I lumber up to the woman who was at a party at the house of someone I can't remember where I got hit by someone I can't recall and left with a person I'm not confident I've ever met.

— Hi Julie. Eric. Eric Hardy

Julie eyes me warily and pauses and I'm momentarily fearful that there has been a transgression on my part in our relationship. Therefore I'm considerably relieved when she leans forward to whisper in my ear. Unfortunately:

— If you fucking ever come near me again I'll bite your fucking cheeks off, you son of a bitch.
— Well there's my answer. Looks like I fucked up at the party. Sorry Julie.
— Fuck off you arsehole.
— Okey-dokey.
— That was short.

Says Sam when I return to the table.

— You must have fucked up.
— Must have. Still . . . it couldn't have been too bad. She's still talking to me. Hang on, I've just noticed something. That was a look.
— What was a look?

Asks Jules by way of response to my sound and likely observation.

— That was a look. The woman by the pool cues just gave me a look.
— What, a *look* look?
— I think a *look* look.
— Well go and talk to her.

I'm making the wrong decisions and even at the time there's a whisper somewhere way back deep in the back of my brain trying vainly to alert me that wrong decisions are being made. After four drinks the bit that stores stuff like the name of that film based on the Evelyn Waugh novel and with Alec Guinness in it at the end shut down. After nine drinks the brain bit that organises my holding beers without dropping them and operating cigarette lighters logged off. And at about this point, another five half-spilled drinks later, the bit that allows me to register and correctly process information has closed operations for the evening. I'm in a parallel universe where big red sweaty drunk guys are appealing and exactly the sort of thing that unknown women would like to spend time with.

— That was a look.

I say.

— I beg your pardon?

She says.

— That was a look. Before . . . when we made eye contact . . . that was a look. Hello, my name's Eric. Your look. That was a look wasn't it?
— Fuck Off!!
— I so completely beg your pardon.
— Fuck-Off-Cunt!!
— Well this is shambolic.
— Why is this is shambolic Fuckhead?
— I so thought you gave me a look.
— Just fuck off. Why don't you just fuck off.
— And though you're ugly I thought it would at least be gallant of me to acknowledge the look and at least feign interest.

At this point she throws her drink over me.

I walk back to Sam and Jules and um . . . I lick around my mouth and swab the side of the face and then taste my fingers, discerning and identifying her drink as Fra

Angelico and vodka, which is kind of flattering. If a woman's not going to sleep with you it is a nice consolation prize to know she wasted a fairly expensive drink in expressing her disgust.

— How did that go?

Asks Sam.

— Good. I think good. I think it was a Nut-rush.
— Well that's up on the iced waters and beers you usually get drenched with.
— Yep. They're about $6.50 aren't they?
— About that. Go and talk to her again.
— I think I will.

Things pretty much roll on from here to their preordained conclusion. The beer the cigarettes and the shouting oneself hoarse. The being elbowed in the back and the spilling the drink on the woman and apologising and then wiping down the table and knocking it over. The leering at the cleavage of the woman playing pool and then being told to fuck off by her boyfriends. Chewing gum bought at a time when I foolishly thought anyone might care what my breath smelt like is fumbled with and dropped. Festering socks and sweat stains under the arms and beer on the belly and post-urinal drip smears on the pants. More beer, bigger beer. More Scotch, bigger Scotch and then boom even I figure I've got to go and I announce to Sam and Jules that it's probably time I hastily enact my departure.

— Well . . . look. Things being such as they are, and things being such that they are, I think perhaps I might hastily enact my departure.

NIGHT ON GORE STREET

— See you.
— Bye.

Without a word of protestation. Well fuck them. I'm off.
Suck the milk of the whore of Satan, you arsewipes, I
think to myself, and then conclude it's a more powerful
sentiment if audibly verbalised.
— Well fuck you. I'm off. Suck the milk of the whore
of Satan you arsewipes.
— Yep. Will do. See-you.
— Bye.

I push against the bit that's a door.

And so, after at greater length having announced my
intention to depart than it took to enact that departure, I
ineptly (though with enough force to cover the actual lack
of skill I bring to the action) force open the doors to the
pub and thrust and heave my six-foot-four of mismatched
and uncooperative bulk out and into the night.

Well that's a rush.
If that ain't sobering nothing is.
As a result of the sudden attention the cold breeze pays to
my pub-warmed nose, and the mind-clearing effect of the
clear air on my smoke-clouded eyes and the more urgent
clambering my testicles made into and upward to the
warmth of my body, I am momentarily able to sober up
enough to vomit, and then establish in what direction I
live.

If this was a competition sport—and getting six-foot-four
drunk guys home from the pub late at night *should* be a

competition sport (hell I'd go and see it) I'd back Hardy to get himself there.

The man moves like a gazelle.

A nice little flick-the-vomit-off-the-lapel-while-bumping-into-the-tree there. Always stylish, always cool.

A well executed piss-on-the-shop-front-while-grinding-the-forehead-mercilessly-into-the-brickwork manoeuvre.

'Very popular with the Mexican judge but not so popular with the Eastern Europeans—such a mainstay of Yeltsin's routine that they've all grown a bit weary. He might have lost valuable points there.'

Oh—and oh—a superb fall over the bonnet of the car while still spilling urine and trying to hail a cab that already has passengers. And he finishes by hitting his head heavily on the road surface. Well that's why Hardy is competing at this level—if you want to know how drunk fucking losers get themselves home from the pub well, this guy wrote the book, and it makes me proud to be an Australian.

Feeling pretty close to having peaked, I resort to that hoary old chestnut, that traditional crowd pleaser, that ever reliable, cry in the gutter for twenty minutes.

Which I happily do. I don't know who I am cursing. I don't know who has transgressed. I don't know why I am so sad. But it certainly seems fitting that I cry in abject self pity for about twenty minutes until I realise three things—

A)- The whole stumble, piss, hail thing has left me with very wet trousers and they are now becoming sticky and discomforting.

B)- As mentioned above, I have completely forgotten what was upsetting me and therefore I could continue without giving it further address.

C)- My primary objective is getting my sweet buns home and I am in no way serving this purpose by sitting in a gutter in my urine crying about someone I may well have never met.

With considerable strength and application—and if you've been there you'll admire my resolution (if you've ever seen that kerbside tyre you'd understand how eminently curl-up-against-and-cuddleable it is) I stagger myself up and get the left foot-right foot thing going until I bump into a park.

As I walk through the park, eyes focused on my feet until I'm fairly confident that they're going to be able to continue the left-right forward thing without my mindful scrutiny, I decide I'm actually ready to diversify operations and add to my performance a bit of looking up and seeing where I'm actually going. Despite carefully pacing the straightening of the neck, the refocusing of the eyes, one at a time, the moving the head a bit from left to right, the whole enterprise is a disaster. The feet are hopeless without my attention, jealous and piqued, my body goes into shock, and I fall into a bush.

Bummer. I sit up, laugh for a while until I remember that I've fallen into a bush.

A dark shape walks past with the lumbering gait of a male, looks at me quickly, scratches his balls and keeps walking. He stops about thirty metres further along, stands for a moment under a lamppost and then walks by again, scratches his balls and keeps walking. And then a third time.

— What on earth are you doing?

I say.

— What?
— Are you lost.
— No.
— Well you just keep walking by and doing that half-scratch thing? Is that a secret code? 'The microfilm is hidden under the clock tower' sort of thing? I don't think I'm your contact just quietly.
— What are you talking about?
— I'm wondering why you keep on . . . Oh. I see. Are you courting me? But . . . I'm a drunk idiot in a bush. What on earth are you thinking?

He sits down next to my bush and starts fumbling for a cigarette, looking around nervously.

— So . . . What's your name sir?
— What?
— Your name. I was wondering what your name was? My name's Eric. Eric Hardy.
— John.
— Hello John. John What?
— John Brown.
— You're kidding. Kind of dull. Kind of dull and generic. Oh I see . . . you *are* kidding. We exchange semen and small flecks of faecal matter but we're very careful about keeping our names to ourselves. That's the etiquette here is it, it's um . . . what do you do? Do you work? Were you working tonight? I was just wondering. Like . . . were you on your way home from work and thought—MacDonald's?

    Hmmm . . . No. A coke maybe, a drink . . . No. Maybe I'll go and suck on some stranger's cock in the park . . . Mmm, that'd be just the thing.

— Fuck off.

— Do you have any kids of your own John?

— Fuck up.

— No seriously . . . I'm interested. Do they know daddy sucks cocks in parks. Do you have a shot at the other dads at father and son barbeques?

If I didn't understand the exchange of names bit about doing a beat I soon learnt that I'd seriously misunderstood the idle conversation bit. So having obviously faux pas-ed in some way, John Brown called me a cunt, walked off, returned with a steering wheel lock and beat the shit out of me. He called over three guys who were also walking through the park and told them that I'd tried to suck his cock, and they beat the shit out of me too. The possums who had witnessed the whole thing and could have testified in my defence must have summed up the whole situation and wisely kept mum.

So that was my excellent Saturday night. I got home and sat in the bath for four hours and cried, this time with an identifiable reason. I went back to my parents for a couple of days and just told them I'd got in a blue at a pub and played on dad's computer. By Thursday I was ready to work and yesterday I worked a half shift. Today I just idled, listened to the footy and I've just watched The Simpsons. (The 'George Bush moves in across the road' episode. Does life get better that this?)
I'm sick of typing and I guess I'll give Sam and Jules a call.

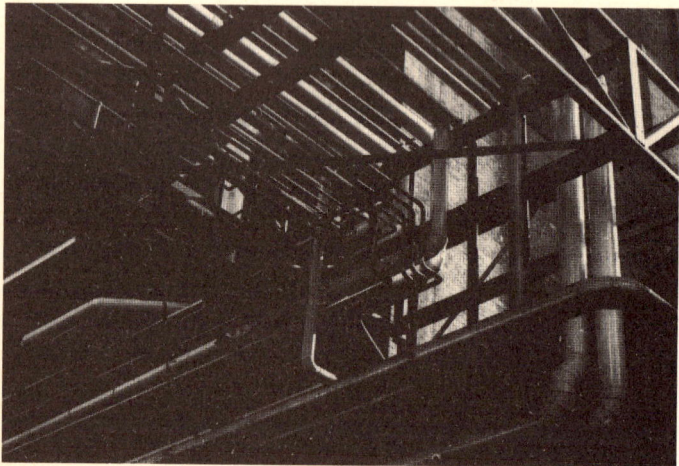

THE MONITORS

Bernard Cohen

I give warning that I shall not here give the essence of every perception. I shall confine myself to the character of fictitious, false, and doubtful perception, and the means of freeing ourselves therefrom.

Benedict de Spinoza,
On the Improvement of the Understanding

We stand around the microtome, which has broken down halfway through sectioning a batch of onion skin-thin liver tissue. I think the fault is in the belt mechanism, but Colin believes the blade has come loose. Eric tells us that the last person to know everything was the philosopher Liebniz, and he died in 1716. The surface of the only cover-slipped slide seems to be painted in brilliant, fluorodescent hues of green-yellow and red. The tissue resembles a compound of hornet, grasshopper and shrimp cells, magnified enormously. Not good. Dye extrusion fault?

'Put out a press release headed "New species: Techo's chance discovery", and send it over to Bacteriology,' Colin suggests.

Too late. I've discarded the slide and started systematically working back along the conveyor. One-two-three, perfectly trained. I do not respond to Colin, but tell Eric, 'You mean Western knowledge.'

Eric retorts: 'Is there any other kind?'

Colin starts listing, naming Caribbean and Pacific islands or Asian nations after each piece of information.

'Right-o. Enough,' Eric snaps.

'You would say that, anyway,' Colin tells him, shirtily.

'Big deal,' says Eric and exaggerates his slight French-Belgian accent to quote the relevant European thinker: ' "A body without soul is a body assisted by technical prostheses." '

'Yeah,' says Colin. 'Right.'

Eric's lips draw into a slow-mo sneer as he readies himself to continue, but an alarm signal from 2B terminates the conversation. Eric and I rush out, Colin follows with the toolbox.

Later, at the pub, Colin comments, 'I bet that Liebniz guy didn't know many folk songs.'

I'm not yet too drunk, and am still trying to balance loyalties. I say, 'He spoke ninety-four European languages.'

'Sure he did. Listen to this,' he commands, pulling a dog-eared volume of Nino Majellaro poetry from his coat pocket, pretending he's just thought to read it to me: ' "The water that beats down with the persistence of a metronome and makes dough of the houses is like the daily paper, it's a sodden idea that our minds can be purged of prejudices." '

I can hardly drag my eyes from the pub screen, where impressionistic dogs charge around the pixilated track.

' "Sodden"?' I say.

Next night, observing the operation from Monitor Room One, the pub TV scene repeats.

'This signal must have gone through a blender,' Eric complains.

'Press RGB. That'll clarify it,' I suggest.

'Watch it on the small monitor, for Chrissake,' Colin mumbles, but tries to fix the picture anyway.

'Can we have some volume? The sound. No, a little more, not yet.'

'Yeah, that's it for sound.'

'It's not real clear, is it?' Colin backs away to get a better view. 'Can hardly make out a goddam thing, not that I can see past the end of my nose in the first place.'

The surgeon's become entirely blue, clothes, skin, hair. In fact, everything's blue and no-one else seems to notice or, if they do, it doesn't bother them. I imagine some old-time supervisor growing: 'My boy, this would irritate the crap out of you if you were competent.'

But there is no supervisor. We are responsible for ourselves. (First-year training manual, Introduction.) Now Colin's found us some colour, but the red's come apart from the green.

'How many lines per inch are you supposed to get on this fucking thing?' Eric gripes. 'Can't you adjust it, like move the screen forward or something? It's really hard to see. Flip to the other circuit maybe.'

'You ought to relax, mate. What channel are you on, anyway?' This from the orderly, who shouldn't even have been there. 'Or are you right off the air?'

Colin comes close to losing it. He's concentrating on the wiring, as he always does when the signal falls apart. He's holding four or five different screws between his lips, and loops of wire are hooked around his neck. He glares at the orderly, who couldn't have any idea what's involved, but says nothing to him. Finally the picture's good enough: the whirr of surgical hands like greyhounds across the patient's yellow-pink chest.

I'm filling in time with self-accusations and self-confessions. Work is damaging. The constant pauses provide too much space for abstractions: 'I acknowledge a great fear of anything that will distract me from my studies or interfere with my habits. I am overcome by spasms of depth/shallowness, by the constant recession of the multiplying image, by smoke and the stink of beer. I am lost in the invisibility of that big, falling-apart screen.'

The whole surgical-video thing washes over me in giant waves of fatigue. Our beery, bleary eyes unconsciously disencode the red/green and assemble an entire . . . oh, who knows what we'd see? The orderly tries to be funny, but he's not. It's pretty straightforward, this operation, not much more than an exploratory. The orderly, in a nasal whine, takes up the call: 'And there she is, her offsider is hosing the mud off, she's ready for it again and the barracker beside me really believes this is competitive sport, he really believes observing this is analogous to watching the operation of class society, he really hopes the snobby bitch pins her.'

'For Chrissake,' says Colin.

'On that size monitor,' says the orderly, 'you could miss the whole pointillism.'

Meanwhile, I had learned to see the actual flesh on the actual screen and cannot stop interpreting these pictures. Would Sir Thomas More pick up the idea as quickly as we seem to have—I mean, once he got over the shock of being transported through time and all that? Does an Ancient Egyptian see the paintings around Luxor as likenesses? Or some other form of representation? If a machine is programmed to print 'I am in state A' when in state A, how does this differ from Jones saying, 'I am in pain' (or something as automatic) when in pain? I'm too caught up in the patient's feelings, says the debriefing counsellor. I'm supposed to chant, 'I want none of this involvement' or something. I ought to want to watch the procedure, for it to be over with, and return to the cedar-veneer saloon bar for the salt on the peanuts, the satyriasic cartoon kickboxers, and the young man in front of me in the betting queue, rasping 'My lover doesn't love me' to the betting shop attendant, watching the attendant's eyes as she hands over the last blue ticker of this day's losing streak, and her fingers briefly touch his palm, her face illegible.

It rarely turns out to be so simple. I hardly ever leave on time. This building, despite its apparent solidity, merely masks the circuitry: it's a proto-hospital of copper wiring and optical fibres. We move from filament to filament checking that this invisible substance functions even while the false, voluminous hospital smothers the patients and their visitors with insincere reassurance. Every procedure here is driven by finely calculated allowances for mechanical failure and the infinite shades of human error, so that whether the scalpel enters just here, or a micron further over, the patient will live. If the probability of survival (S) drops below a certain level, depending on the procedure, the surgeon's skill and experience and the patient's prior health indicators—all factors with readily available pronumerals—laser is substituted for metal. Signal fibres pass between the walls through narrow, temperature-stabilised tubes. Wires staple-gunned above the ceiling lead to green-whirring fluorescent tubes. Finer filaments, stretched out under our feet as we half-run between monitor rooms, send little green wave-patterns across tiny green monitors. This sense of the hospital has absolutely cancelled out the masonry for me. It's a predatory logic which once acknowledged cannot be set aside. My job becomes holding up the building, divining every hint of metal fatigue. Any screen-flicker could be significant. My shift finishes, but work goes on and on.

Eric leans forward, presses the green button and says evenly to the pick-up, 'We've got no channel three. Repeat. We've got a problem with channel three.'

I get his voice distorting back at me through the headphones like he's a badly tuned radio. The white gowns converge on the torso, totally obscuring my view of the prone figure. Not that it matters; I've got other things to keep an eye on. They're swinging arms, pumping, counting out loud, flipping electrodes to 'on'. At four-second intervals, someone yells, 'Now!'

The volume of the shout is way outside my headphones' capability. It's all attack. I'm trying to shake the noise out of my ears without removing the 'phones, as a row of minuscule, yellow-glass hemispheres lights up in front of me.

'Yellow's on,' I proclaim.

'Gotcha,' says Eric, instead of 'thanks'. But he doesn't do anything until he sees it on his own screen. When it's okay, he presses the green button again and says, 'That channel's firing. Repeat. Channel three's happening just fine.'

At the pub Colin is explaining the ontological distinction between video projection and television. The pub screen is behind him. On it, spotty anglers reel in spotty fish with grotesque jaws; interspersed are close-ups of lures and thirty-second lessons in attaching hooks to lines. I'm filling the space between beer-swallows saying 'Mm, mm' to Colin whenever he says 'y'know?' and going to the bar every other time we drain our glasses. I hate watching these people fishing, but I just cannot concentrate to listen to Colin. I beg the bartender to change channels and she says 'Yeah, just a minute,' but does nothing because she guesses I'll soon be too drunk to care. I'm trying to argue with her. I'm saying, 'I always care. Always.'

She smiles.

'I can tell, mate. I really can,' she says.

I find myself going over and over all the material we're supposed to know. All this 'wow, I'm so covert' stuff about getting secrets that never should have been secret anyway across to the other side. You know the plot: 'I met Roschinsky at the Hotel Nord at 7 p.m., and he handed me the sheaf with the antidote formula. Glancing at it, I immediately knew it was false. There was no nausea suppressant anywhere in the list of ingredients. Earlier, in Berlin, 1965, we found the Russians had blocked up the pinhole for our probe microphone.'

The old surgeons think the comprehensive approach is wonderful, so different from what they went through, and especially the cameras and fucking condenser mikes all over theatre. They love it: they think it's real C21 spy tech. I think every senior doctor in the place has anecdoted me about the mnemonics he or she devised to remember the musculature of the hand for the final examinations. They tell me how much more profound it is to have literary allusions and stories about leeches and barber-surgeons who made genuine medical advances despite adversity and near-total lack of hygiene.

Still, I'm in no position to feel superior to them: I spend some nights in the monitor room, fall asleep with the headphones humming the dark, noiseless surgeries into my head. I dream all these lines of coloured lights, patterns blinking and, in these dreams, I understand what the patterns are saying. We're having a conversation, the lights and I.

What does this mean I want? I love my work? I wish I'd studied semaphore? Someone wrote, probably as an epigraph, 'A compulsive thought is really a compulsive deed and the surrogate for an action.'

For a few moments, as I lose consciousness, I come to believe that the theatres are not constituted by the cuttings-up and measuring. Because the operating theatres can be silent, work remains possible. And I'm asleep.

What's most bizarre is what the patients must make of hospitalisation, surgery, ritual care: all the bindings-in, the probes and pick-ups taped all over their bodies like sacramental medallions. They're lying there, absolutely loaded with IV morphine, sliding along hundreds of metres of Arctic White corridors. They must be flipping out, as in: 'The wind picked up, flicking droplets of rain, sweat, oil through the wire mesh. I walked up Death Row for the last time, turned into the execution chamber, and was strapped into the Chair by two guards I had never seen before.'

Of course, I could be projecting my own horror at death written in dozens of electronic signal failures. It's reasonable, says the counsellor, and I'm trying to explain that Reason is the whole problem, but I haven't got the vocabulary.

And then the patients are out, but the brain activity continues. We're sitting there in the fucking monitor room, and the little screen keeps flickering. We can see someone's in there, blood laced with all these demi-poisons, and they're still producing millions of brainwaves. We're supposed to keep an eye on it, and we do, but what can you really know? All these squiggly lines on the monitor have to correspond to something: 'Thousand of years pass on Tharda. The forces of change conspire against the planet's rocky surface, cracking and grinding mountains to boulders, boulders to sand.'

If only those probes were a little more sensitive. This is how to see the world without leaving Australia . . . at the early opener, guitars strumming away in the background, the station logos beckoningly personal. No wonder Liebniz was so confident. He must have had it right: '*Omnia jam fient; fieri quae posse negabam.* Everything will now happen which I declared to be impossible.'

CREEPY CRAWL

Leonie Stevens

At 10.47 I walked into the Stork Hotel with Violet, and we looked pretty good if I say so myself. Violet was wild as always, exaggerated make-up, bra and kilt, purple mohawk rising one clear foot above her head. I tailed behind, less animated in attire but feeling cool 'cause the scab had come off my tattoo and I had Bangers and Mash on my bicep forever.

'Looks great,' Violet said over her shoulder, letting go of the door so it slammed into my arm. A few days ago, when the tat was healing, it would have sent me into screams of agony, but today the chimps smiled back, clear and colourful and permanently set.

'I know,' I said proudly, 'something different.'

'Much more fun than those boys and their Black Flag bars.'

'Did you see Crackers' one?'

'Prison job or what?'

'The bars were round the wrong way.'

'Dya tell him?'

'Are you kidding?'

Her next words were lost in the noise of the bar. It was a typical scene, the early opener crowd four hours into drinking, suss-looking Market yobs strewn around the tables and carpet that permanently smelt of beer. Every face turned on our arrival, and they gave us a warm reception.

'Fuck, look at that!'

'What *are* you?'

'Bloody hell!'

'Piss off!'

'Jeez you're ugly.'

Violet bent over in a fuck you curtsy, rising above the aggravation. I didn't find it so easy. It's one thing to provoke disbelief when you wear something outrageous. People giggle at you, think you're a dill and go back to whatever they're doing. That's okay, that's how we see THEM most of the time. But there's certain types, and I know them well, sick ones who seethe like they wanna smash our faces for not playing the pretty-hair pretty-clothes game.

'Charming, hey?' said Violet, beaming at hostile faces.

'They reckon *we're* anti-social.'

'Shall we get a drink?'

'Without delay.'

'Ten, nine, eight . . .' We made our way through the sea of scattered tables. A grim-faced woman in a loose floral shirt watched our approach to the bar. '. . . three, two, one, lift-off.'

'Houston control, we have ignition.'

'But do we have service?'

The barmaid gave us a stony grunt, like we were subhuman and only law prevented her from pulling out the gun she undoubtedly kept under the counter and putting, as the Angry Samoans sang, our lights out.

'Pot,' said Violet, grinning, 'Thanks.'

'Yeah,' I added, 'same here, please.'

As she grudgingly filled our pots from the tap, I detected some above-average hissing from a guy to my left. He was pissed and nasty, and I knew if we stayed he'd get off his chair to start something, but it's a funny thing. I didn't care any more.

'Hey,' I said, shit-scared and loving it, 'you got something to say?' Violet nudged me in encouragement, 'cos usually she baited the aggro types and I was the one yelling, 'Shit, did you HAVE to do that?' as we ran away.

'Huh?' grunted our tormentor, back stiffening, nervous about how to take this. A girl answering back in front of his mates and all. The indignity!

'D'you reckon he can talk?' I asked.

'Nah,' Violet said, 'he just makes animal noises.'

He stood up suddenly, as if to pounce, sweaty in a blue striped track suit.

'Better hold it right there,' Violet told him.

'Yeah,' I added, 'we know something *you* don't know.'

And we were face-to-face with the shit-in-a-tracksuit when sixty of our closest friends exploded into the pub. They came through three doors at once, a sea of studs and piercings and paint-on leather, shouting and laughing like a single messy organism. The noise level rose to deafening. The market yobs went into deep crisis.

'Hah,' I said to Violet, 'justice.'

'Bugger justice,' she replied, eyes scanning the crowd. 'Justice ain't gonna get me going.'

'Be patient.' I turned to the heckler, still frozen in his pissy tracksuit. 'Didn't you have something to say?'

He stared for a second then sat down with his beer-swilling buddies, all staring at the laminex. Violet went off in search of stimulation, and I hung at the bar for a while, gloating, capitalising on a rare moment of revenge.

'Were they hassling you?' said Heck, protector of the downtrodden seeing as he'd sworn not to drink this time. Not after last year's debacle with Ginny, the V-dub and those lethal rubber pants.

'Them?' I said, pointing to the tracksuit and his grimy mates. 'Nah, ya gotta pity them.'

Heck grinned. 'Do ya?'

'So insecure.'

'What, penis size?' They all squirmed.

'It's gotta be it.'

'They're lucky, though.'

I sipped my beer. 'How's that?'

'Well, this is only number four. By nineteen or twenty, we might not be so charitable.'

We laughed at their expense then rapidly lost interest. The crowd massed around the bar and we had to move or be trampled by endless pairs of scruffy GPs. Heck lit a beedie and we were heading to a table when Brisbane Tim appeared out of nowhere and knocked the beedie flying.

'Wow, this is fantastic!' he enthused, hanging over Heck's shoulder, six foot three of studs and black leather. Tim's hair was bared down to a number one since the unfortunate incident last Tuesday when someone set fire to his mohawk. He used hairspray, and I always told him, stay away from fucking hairspray. I even gave him my hair gel recipe—gelatin sachet, some glycerine, a little aftershave and water, so strong you can't even *wash* it out. But he persisted with hairspray. Some people just won't be told.

'I've never seen anything like this,' he said, probably echoing the thoughts of the straights around the bar. 'It's amazing! It's incredible!'

'Hey, Tim,' Heck said. 'It's just a pub crawl.'

'Yeah, but—oh! It's amazing! Two weeks ago if someone had'a told me we'd be hanging out like this I woulda said sure, in the lock-up.'

Heck raised an eyebrow. 'There's still time.'

'It's fantastic!' Tim raved on, oblivious. 'I can't believe how friendly everyone is down here. Like you guys—you don't even know me and you let me move in.'

'Right place, right time,' Heck said.

'Yeah,' I added, 'we only found the squat last week.' But Tim wasn't having this Reason thing. He was gonna put us on a pedestal whether we liked it or not.

'You've all been so nice, so generous, even when I ate all the chocolate bars, and I want you to know I really really appreciate it—'

We let him blubber on for a while, because it was kind of touching. At seventeen, he'd been bastardised by representatives of every level of society. You name 'em, they'd beaten him up. When he finally made the break, a cheapo bus from Brisbane to Melbourne, he was befriended at the DSS by a sicko coming down off acid—me. I saw the writing on the back of his jacket— LIFE IS SO UGLY, WHY NOT GO KILL YOURSELF—and thought, hmmm, here's a fellow traveller. I took him back to the squat and the place had been caked in slush ever since.

'I really love you guys—'

'Dag,' I said. 'Know where to get any go, then?'

Tim blinked and shook his head, and I continued the mission I'd been on since 8 a.m., when Violet and I crossed town to Punt Road to see if anyone there had connections. Alas, Craig'd gone straight for five minutes, Steve's man got busted last week and the Smith twins were cycling round the country or something. Violet's panic was infectious. There were twenty-three pubs to get through, and I helped print up the fliers, so damned if I was gonna conk out by number 13. Desperate times call for desperate measures. I went up to Rob Hansen.

'Oh,' he said, 'hi.' He was looking me straight in the eye, and I knew he'd been badmouthing me all round town, saying I was a stupid cow or a conniving bitch. He saw me as a severe threat because I got a letter in Maximum Rock 'n' Roll and his faster-than-the-speed-of-light band couldn't get a mention, not even when the guitarist blew his brains out. But what the hell. It was pub crawl day. Temporary truce.

'What you been up to?' I said, wanting to add, 'Except slagging me off.' His eyes flickered around the bar, hoping no-one saw us together.

'Oh, lookin' for a new guitarist.'

'Fuck, that was bad news about Vinnie.'

'Shit yeah,' Rob muttered. 'It's fucked.' His lips barely moved. 'Know where to get any go?'

That's just what I was gonna ask him. 'Uh-uh. Violet reckons that guy Jason can get on.'

His eyes rolled. 'What the fuck would she know?'

I wanted to tell him, 'She thinks you're cute! That's how little *she* knows!' Oh, there was so much I wanted to say to Rob, but I'd sworn not to sink to his level. Smiling, holding it back Oriental-style, I told him I'd let him know if I heard of anything, then joined the 11.15 exodus to pub number four.

It was still early, and people were merry and matey and not-too-drunk, except for Tim, who was blubbering ad nauseam to anyone who'd listen. I saw him trying to keep up with Nancy, who set a cracking pace despite being so close to term that it made everyone nervous.

'Wow,' Tim was saying, marvelling at her pregnant swollenness, 'your stomach's so *huge*.'

Her boyfriend Jessie said 'Der!' Nancy smiled patiently. I dodged a half-dozen dancing dogs to get close to her.

'How long you got to go?' I asked.

'Who knows?' she said, green eyes so glazed and satisfied that you'd swear she'd just had smack or an orgasm. All those hormones. 'It was due three days ago.'

'All this walking might bring it on,' I suggested, thinking Elizabeth Street on a Saturday morning wasn't the optimum place to go into labour.

'That's the idea,' she said, almost tripping on a kelpie. 'I was running up and down stairs all yesterday, trying to induce it.'

'And you moved that wardrobe,' Jessie added.

'Yeah, it was bloody heavy.'

'That's 'cause Eddie was in it.'

Nancy turned to me with an electric smile. She was so pure and pretty, she had no place being on a pub crawl. 'My brother hitched down from Mudgeedonga. He was gonna surprise me—'

'What, jump out and frighten a pregnant woman?'

'Yeah.' Her eyes beamed proudly. 'Sweet, huh? But he fell asleep, the slack bastard. I moved the wardrobe round to block off the fireplace, 'cause all this soot keeps blowing in and I wanted to get it all clean for the baby, then a couple of hours later we're out in the yard and Vicki comes out and says, shit, there's something really weird going on in your room. He'd been knocking—he couldn't get out.'

Jessie struck a pose and sang 'He ain't heavy . . .' Nancy jabbed him in the ribs. I scanned the crowd as we bounced towards the next pub, ever on the look out.

'So did he come today?'

She nodded and looked around. 'Yeah. He's here somewhere.'

Jessie burst into laugher and made scratching motions, croaking 'Let me out, let me out.' Nancy had to support her belly when she laughed.

The numbers picked up as we walked, late risers who couldn't make it to the Naughten at 10 a.m. At the next pub, a public servant dive from Monday to Friday, kind of purposeless on the weekends, the proprietors gave us welcome, bemused smiles. There was none of the animosity of the Stork. I buzzed around, asking new arrivals if they knew of any go, but most of them said 'No, you?' Heck sat by the window, shaking his head like a green-haired Father Superior.

'Hah!' I called across the bar. 'Like *you* never did anything decadent!' He pointed at me and laughed.

And the pub crawl swaggered along. At number five, Sandra Woe arrived to perform her public ritual. Flanked by a dim boy from Canberra, she bought a pot in each pub in honour of Vinnie, the guitarist with the exploding head. Violet thought I wasn't being sensitive enough.

'She really loved him,' she said, elbows on the bar, still sober enough to be generous. 'I mean—all that stuff about her only being with him 'cause he dealt—I don't think that's true. I mean—so what if it was?'

'Doesn't make it easier to clean.'

Violet turned slowly. 'Huh?'

'The blood—apparently it was all over the walls.' She stared at me intently, and I realised I was drunk. 'What I mean is—even if he was a prick—' She grew more alarmed by the second. 'Shit, I don't know what I mean.'

'Oh.' She nodded happily. 'Look there.'

A big weekend punk in an Exploited T-shirt was hanging around Sandra's table. He tried to be inconspicuous, watching Vinnie's pot, but he was so fake with the colour spray and shiny boots that you couldn't help but notice him. Exploited—huh! After a few minutes he did a pathetic job of trying to nick Vinnie's beer, and Mick, the beefhead from Canberra who'd been hanging around Sandra for years and had Vinnie RIP tattooed on his arm even though he only met him once, jumped on him, yelling 'Hey, that's Vinnie's!' Suddenly everyone in the place was glaring at the Exploited guy, and he kept trying to apologise but Mick was getting hysterical, screaming 'You tryin' to take a beer off a dead man?' Twenty people crowded around to settle Mick down. The Exploited guy grovelled his way out the door and didn't show his face for three pubs.

At number six, the Main Men arrived. Eddie, Crackers and Marty Mauler. We called them the Main Men because they were the biggest, toughest guys on the whole scene. They should carry EXPLOSIVE labels. Put them somewhere risky like, say, a Motorhead covers gig, and there's no telling what could happen. But on pub crawl day, they were a picture of civility.

Eddie looked absolutely frightful. He'd taken up body building, put on a heap of weight then stopped with the exercise, so flab was hanging out his jeans and tight singlet. He asked me if I knew where to get some wiz.

I said 'No, you?', and he gave me a half-baked story about Marty Mauler's sister bringing some in from Dandenong. It couldn't have been too certain, otherwise he wouldn't have been asking me. As I made my way to the ladies', Crackers and Marty Mauler nabbed me.

'Got any David Bowie?'

'Got any Margaret Mead?'

The Margaret Mead thing threw me for a moment. Maybe Crackers was a secret anthropologist. I told them I'd keep them informed and left them in their tight corner, cos these were volatile individuals. The other night Marty stormed through Punt Road with an axe, screaming 'Where's Crackers? I'm gonna kill him.' Two days later, they were slamming tequila like that Temaze never went missing. The pub crawl was a great leveller.

At number seven, I took a candid photo of Karl Kick jumping over the bar to steal a beer, thinking I could blackmail him one day. Ordinarily, Karl is the biggest pain-in-the-arse straight-edge dude in town. All-singing, all-lecturing, his disapproval list even extended to caffeine and sex.

'You get that on film?' Heck asked me, materialising out of nowhere as Karl found a hiding spot for his demon drink.

'Yeah—who'd believe it otherwise?'

'I bet you cut his head off.'

'Great! We can call him Vinnie!'

'Sssshhh.' We bobbed our heads in mock seriousness. 'I mean, you can't blame the guy.'

'Who, Vinnie? He pulled the trigger.'

'No, Karl.'

'What, *he* pulled the trigger?'

Heck made a playful swipe. 'You know what I mean.'

CREEPY CRAWL

Yes, the Kickstart thing. The sad dissolution of one of the best bands in Melbourne because—oh, the ig-nominy—the singer became a cop. Karl was devastated.

'Poor guy,' I said. 'Maybe he's reinventing himself.'

'What, to beer-stealing hero?'

'I saw him riding a skateboard yesterday.'

'What a suck!'

'You're just jealous cos you're unbalanced.'

Heck squinted. 'It's an inner ear thing.'

On the way out of pub number eight, I heard the cry of 'Look! It's Jason!', and suddenly this straight-looking little guy who no-one paid attention to before today was surrounded by mates asking if he could get some speed. And he was organised, good for it, keeping track of all the orders, so I gave him the forty bucks I'd scraped together and he promised to be back soon. Demented with excitement, Violet gave him a map and tried to work out which pub we'd be at on his return, but he just laughed and said he found us by asking someone in the street, 'Hey, did you see a big crowd of punks go by?', and ten people said 'That-a-way', so it shouldn't be too hard.

And then he was gone.

And we were all waiting again.

At pub number nine, a beautiful Gothic girl walked in and Crackers, who was sitting next to me, just about died. She looked around the bar and set sights on a friend, and the two of them sat together, on their own, nervous cos they didn't seem to know anyone. Out of the good-ness of my heart, and because I was too drunk to know better, I struck up a conversation with them—hairdress-ers, of course—then Crackers took over. By number ten, they were getting closely acquainted, and at number eleven, Crackers was walking round in a daydream

215

asking everyone 'Have you seen that *girl*?' Everyone knew who he meant but no-one could help. I tried to tell him that the course of love doesn't always run smoothly, especially on a pub crawl, but then I caught sight of one of Rob Hansen's hateful stares across the landscape of spikes and studs, and every ounce of optimism drained from my body.

Bloody Rob.

The rot set in, beer-tiredness.

I made it outside before I burst into tears, cos I didn't want to give him the satisfaction. I was somewhere on Russell Street—fuck knows, I lost track three pubs ago—and all I wanted to do was go home. I hid in a lane. Not very well.

'Hey, what are you doing here?'

I looked up and saw Nancy, a vision of nature framed by rotting posters and garbage, clean and pretty and wise.

'I can't stand it any more.'

She squatted down next to me with some difficulty. 'Can't stand what?'

Down on the street, the pub crawl was mobile. I watched hundreds of legs in ripped jeans and stockings and associated dogs march up the hill. They all knew about Rob's backstabbing, but what did they do? Some friends.

'Them,' I said, noticing Rob go by with Marty Mauler and Eddie, all best mates and testosterone.

'Why? What happened?'

I sucked my knees to my chin and surrendered to sadness. 'Nothing new.'

'What, was Rob at it again?'

I sniffed and nodded. 'How did you know?'

'Don't worry about it. No-one listens to him.'

'No-one tells him to shut up, either.' Nancy took a

deep breath and patted her stomach, like the baby was kicking to get out. I put my head in my hands and said, 'Sorry. You don't need this.'

'You shouldn't let him get to you.'

I heard footsteps and Heck's voice saying 'Who?'

'Rob,' Nancy told him. 'He's getting out of line.'

Heck took my hands away from my face and said, 'I thought you didn't care.'

'Of course I don't care! Why would I care? No-one gives a fuck.'

'Oh.' Heck paused for a while. 'I can hear the violins. No friends. No-one cares.'

I wanted to cry. 'That's right.'

'Well, except maybe that time you were in hospital.'

I looked at him. 'Huh?'

'That's when I met you. Crackers said, come on, you gotta come and meet this girl.'

'Yeah,' Nancy added, 'you told me that you got so many visitors it made you sick.'

I nodded. 'You're right.'

'And when that skinhead punched you in the mouth down at the Prince Patrick, and all the bands got together—'

I'd fogotten about that. 'Yeah.'

'And on your birthday.'

'Okay.'

'—and when you got evicted—'

'Alright.'

'—and whenever your cheque's late—'

'Okay! You're right! How many times I gotta say it?'

Heck grinned victoriously. 'God, I hate a crying drunk.'

'Me too,' Nancy said, and she put her hand out for Heck to help her up. As they left the lane, Nancy round and full and Heck thin and scruffy, I had to face it. I did have a social security system. Okay, maybe they didn't stick up for me in the face of Rob's rantings, but I'd never starve, or be homeless, or want for a smoke. A smiling kelpie came up, sniffed my knee then tore off up the street. Go dog go. I wiped the tears, staggered to my feet and decided to catch up to the mob at number twelve. I rounded the corner just in time to crash into Jason the fast master.

'Jason!' I squealed. 'How'd you go?'

He patted the pocket of his nondescript shirt, looking like a clean-cut boy scout. 'Mission accomplished.' He bent closer, looking at me closely. 'Are you okay?'

I guess my eyes were still red. I said, 'Yeah. Just tired. Been going since the first pub.'

He looked down the empty street. 'Heaps more people than last year.'

'Yeah.' I studied his face, surprised. 'Were you on it then?'

He grinned. 'Sure. Remember the police helicopter?'

'Yeah—they thought it was a riot.'

'Dickheads.'

I couldn't help staring, trying to place him.

'I used to be really fat,' he said, as if that explained everything. We stood calmly on Russell Street for a moment, like this was a quiet break at a noisy gig, and I thought about appearances and weight loss until I remembered what he was carrying. A rush of excitement propelled me into motion.

'Come on,' I said, pulling his arm, and instead of slinking we *raced* through the streets, going from pub to pub till we found the mob in a place that wasn't even on the map.

'Jason!' everyone screamed, and I got out of the way

because I already had mine. I was looking around for Violet, or someone else to do the job with, when Heck passed by and said 'Brace yourself.' I was about to say 'What for?' when I felt a hand on my shoulder.

'Listen,' Rob said, sincere as a mad bastard can be, 'I just wanna say—I hope we can let bygones be bygones.'

I gaped and said, 'What?'

'I'm sorry if I've been a prick.'

And that was it. I witnessed a miracle. Rob Hansen giving a sincere apology. Everyone I knew was watching. Shit, I wished I had my camera out.

'So anyway, you want to come to the gig tonight?'

It was incredible. Now he was being friendly. Completely thrown, I said, 'Gig? What gig?'

'Down at the Central Club. It'll be great. Heck's gonna fill in on guitar.'

'Er—I dunno—'

'I'll put you on the door.' Then he smiled and walked away. I found Heck in the speed feeding frenzy and said, 'Did you put him up to that?'

'Nah, not me.'

'Bullshit.'

'I may have had a word to Crackers.'

'Thanks.'

'Like I said—I hate to see a crying drunk.'

'I'm not gonna be drunk much longer.' I gave him a glimpse of the folded paper in my palm. 'Want some?'

It didn't take much to tempt him, seeing as he'd been watching everyone else get shit-faced all day. We checked the toilets, but they were full. It looked like half of Melbourne was tanking up. We grabbed a map from one of the tables and left for the next pub, laughing, almost running. We were right on the edge of the city by now, and it was getting dark—all the better.

'I didn't make it this far last year,' I commented as we cut across some traffic.

'Me either,' Heck said, and I couldn't help laughing. Poor Heck. They had to cut his rubber pants off at the hospital. Even though they were stolen, those pants were worth a hundred and seventy-five bucks to someone.

At pub thirteen—or was it fourteen, there were two on the same block and Violet's map wasn't too good to start with—we went straight to the toilets. Outside the cubicle we ran into Crackers' brother David, who must have had the same idea. The three of us crammed into a dunny and I brought out my miniature make-up mirror. I wiped it clean with toilet paper, then we searched for notes, but we were all down to coins. David had his Newstart form, but we thought that might bum out the high, so he went to the bar to get a straw.

'Hey,' Heck said suddenly, 'did you hear about Nancy?'

'What?'

'She went into labour—just after we left you in that lane. She was really calm, and she says to me, oh, I think it's time I was getting to the hospital, can you get Jessie, and by this time everyone's miles away, and I had to run to the top of the hill and scream out JESSIE, and Sandra's a couple of blocks away on top of the next hill, so she yells for him and he bolts down going berserk, and Nancy's totally together, timing the contractions, saying Mmmm, it's not gonna be long—'

There was a knock on the door, and David came back in.

'Did you know she was only fifteen?'

'Who,' I said, 'Nancy?'

'No, Mother Teresa.'

'Of course, I know everything.'

'Did she have her baby?' David asked.

'Dunno.'

'Imagine if she has it before the pub crawl finishes,' David said. 'We could drink to it.'

'As if we need an excuse.'

'It'd be profound. Someone should call the hospital.'

'Hey, did anyone tell her brother?'

Heck shook his head. 'We couldn't find him.'

'Jeez, he's probably locked in a bar fridge somewhere.'

David went first, and we watched him for signs, because he was a ten year veteran and he wouldn't steer us wrong. He snorted it all up like a hungry hog, then grunted 'Oh, yeah—it's good.' Which meant not too strong—that'd be 'Fuuuuuck'—and not too weak—which would be 'Hmmmph.' He scratched the back of his head as it came on, and we fixed ourselves up. Heck snorted his, a little in each nostril, and didn't even wince. I was shuddering from the taste before I even put the straw to my nose. Sniff, up, ouch—it burnt, the foul taste down the back of my throat, and then it rolled through, cool and fast, tingling the tips of my hair. I was totally, overly awake. The guys grinned at each other, and Heck said, 'Right, let's *crawl*!'

Of course, we were much too fast to crawl. We left the pub in time to see a giant mob of punks cross the road with complete disregard for the law. They were loud and raucous, post-Jason, getting up steam for the night ahead. I sat on a bench with Heck and David and watched for a while.

I noticed soppy Tim step up into the main entrance of the next pub. Four yobbos were standing around talking, and in his drunken buffoonery, Tim accidentally bumped one of them. He stepped back, smiled and said 'Sorry, man,' but the man wasn't so forgiving. He grabbed Tim by the collar and started slapping him around.

'Look,' I said to Heck.

'I see it.'

We rose to go to Tim's aid, but before we could get there the Main Men came round the corner. Marty Mauler—who didn't know Tim, but recognised a friend—bailed the offending guy in a headlock against the tiled wall, keeping him dangling till Crackers and Eddie and Michael and Rob joined in, and within ten seconds the guy and his mates were running away and Tim was staring doe-eyed at the Main Men saying, 'Thanks! Thanks! Thanks!', cos he was used to a Saturday night phonebook-beating from the Brisbane cops, and to him Melbourne was the land of milk and honey and extreme non-violence.

He hadn't seen Marty Mauler on pension day.

The next few pubs were a blur. Everyone was fast and friendly, the ones with money shouting those who'd run out, the hand of friendship being extended so that no-one was on their own. Somewhere in Carlton, the hairdresser Goth girl came back, and Crackers just about got on his knees and prayed. I sat with Heck and some under-age Werribee boys, and when we told them they could crash at the squat tonight, it was like we'd revealed some mystical secret. Like wow, these people live in a squat, wacko, when in reality it was just a cold shambles running power from a sympathetic neighbour.

'We may have made a mistake,' Heck whispered at the bar.

'What—the Werribee boys?'

'We'll never get rid of them.'

'Oh, nonsense. Look what they gave me.' I showed him their band's single. Line-drawn cover, unreadable in the muted lighting.

'Jeez,' he said, 'they're organised out there.'

'Yeah, even Rob hasn't put out a single yet.'

'And you reckon he could do it on hot air alone.'

'Look out,' I whispered, because Rob was hanging around, anxious to get to know these Werribee boys. If there's one thing Rob needed—besides two tastes a day— it was a teenage fanclub. He put his arm around my shoulder, all sweat and speed, and implored me to come down to the Central Club to see his band. And he was so over-the-top friendly that I almost forgot.

Then, through the pub window, I noticed Karl Kick wandering slowly down the middle of the road. I heard the car horns blasting, angry traffic sounds, and then it registered.

'Fuck!' I yelled, diving off my stool and barging through the bodies to get outside. Karl was on the tram tracks, waiting to be hit. Mister Positive, begging suicide. I dodged the traffic to reach him.

'Hey, Karl!' I put my arm around him. 'You right?'

'It's all too heavy.' His eyes were glazed, overburdened by world affairs and too much beer.

'Come on,' I said. 'Come back to the footpath.'

I steered him there slowly while a couple of the Werribee boys directed traffic. And even though I'd never had much to do with him before today, I was overwhelmed by the need to look after him, make sure he got home okay.

'It's not *that* bad,' I told him, knowing full well that on the other 364 days it's worse. Karl sniffed.

'There's just no point.'

'Um—excuse me.' One of the bright-eyed Werribee boys was at my side. His name was Macka or Dacka or something he'd probably change. 'Is there anything I can I do?'

I stared at him—so clean cut—and something weird happened in my brain. It was as if all the acid I ever dropped flashed back. Instant insanity with a passing tram, bodies leaning toward the road, missiles flying through the dull blue yellow, that dancing smiling kelpie again, this time a giant, uninvited and fucking scary for two seconds like centuries. Then I was back and, despite the disorientation, I knew exactly what had happened. You gotta expect *some* craziness on pub crawl day. Macka or Dacka was waiting for a response.

'Coffee,' I said, expelling the flashback breath. 'White with sugar.' I remembered Karl. 'Better get him one too.' My hand went to my pocket, and Macka said 'No', and we had a ridiculous tussle over who was going to pay for the coffee. Karl joined in, emptying the contents of his wallet onto the footpath.

'Take it all,' he said, 'I don't want it.'

'What are you doing?' I yelled, horrified as notes began to blow away. '*Catch that money!*'

Which perhaps was not the wisest thing to do, inviting a streetful of chisellers to grab money, but it got things moving. People and notes flew through the air. Some came back, but most people were pocketing it. Rob came out of the pub and seized control, threatening bodily harm to anyone keeping the currency. Eddie and Marty Mauler stalked the crowd until a few people gave up Karl's money. A few gave up their own, too, but in the face of Marty Mauler after eight hours drinking, who wouldn't?

CREEPY CRAWL

'Here you go.'

Macka was back with a trayful of coffees. We sat on a tram stop and tried to talk to Karl, but he was pretty far gone. Heck came by and made his pronouncement.

'It's the straight ones you gotta watch out for.'

Right on cue, the pub gave up a mass of torn dirty clothes and great hairstyles. Loud voices and screaming colour and yapping dogs clogged the footpath while everyone discussed whether to do the final two pubs.

'It's getting boring—'

'We gotta see it through—'

'Yeah, it's a tradition—'

'Fuck tradition!'

Rob came by the bus stop, and suddenly he was my new best buddy, putting in an earnest effort to redeem himself. He tucked a wad of notes into Karl's pocket and murmured kind words.

'C'arn,' he said to me, 'come down the Central Club.'

'Well . . .' Behind him, Violet was giving wild jerks of encouragement. I lifted the plastic lid, and coffee passed my lips like a tonic. 'Okay.'

And as a group of about forty converged around the tram stop, I thought to myself, we'll have to take Karl with us, make sure he doesn't throw himself under a truck or something. We can all go to the Central Club—the Werribee boys seem keen—and if Karl's still off the planet after that, we can take him back to the squat. Heck might complain in the morning about smelly socks and the milk being used up, but really, even with the Werribee boys and Tim and Violet and whoever else winds up staying, there's always room for one more . . . long as Marty Mauler's got his temaze.

BIOGRAPHIES

Helen Barnes was born on New Years Eve, 1966, and lives in Sydney. Her first novel, *The Crypt Orchid*, was published in 1994. Her second novel, *The Weather Girl*, was published in March 1996.

Neil Boyack was born and adopted in Melbourne, 1967. He has performed with the likes of Jello Biafra, Steve Kilbey, Lydia Lunch amongst others. *See Through* (UQP), is a compilation of his first two books, *Black* and *Snakeskin/Vanilla*, as well as new unpublished work. His work has appeared in many magazines, including the very cool *Eddie*. Neil can be a real asshole and is the frontman sonicsurfuzz guitarist for Melbourne band *CrimeWAVE*. *Jack the Dancer* is part of a new selection of interlinked stories. Neil performs regularly and a spoken word/ambient cassette, *Golden Greats*, is available in cool stores or through the mail.

Bernard Cohen is the author of *Tourism* (Picador, 1992). His second novel, *The Blindman's Hat,* won the 1996 *Australian*/Vogel Literary Award and will be published by Allen & Unwin in September 1997. Among other fiction projects, Bernard is currently writing *The Anti-biography of Robert Fucking Menzies.*

Simon Colvey was born in Melbourne where he currently lives. He has also lived in Montreal and London. A collection of his short stories appears in *See Through* UQP, as well as the small press publications *Black* and *Snakeskin/Vanilla.*

Christopher Cyrill was born in 1970 in Melbourne. His first novel, *The Ganges and its Tributaries*, was published in 1993, and in 1994 he won The Marten Bequest Travelling Scholarship. He has published numerous stories in anthologies and journals and is currently living with the last pages of his next two books, a novel and a book of stories, the title story of which is printed here. He is unconcerned that the London of his imagination does not align with the 'real' London of maps.

Paul Hastie is the author of *Big Things* (Wakefield Press, 1997) and is a collector of snowdomes. He is currently working on event-plans for SCRAM multi-media group, and on an audio project about J-Ward, correctional centre for the criminally insane.

Clare Mendes was born in 1967. Her first novel *Drift Street* won the Angus & Robertson Fiction Prize in 1995 and her second novel *A Race Across Burning Soil* will be published by HarperCollins in 1997. Clare recently adapted *Drift Street* for the screen, and has written for

TV and radio. She has just completed a novel called *The Curtain Raiser*.

Glyn Parry is best known for his writing for teenagers. He has written *LA Postcards* (Random House, 1992), *Monster Man* (Random House, 1994), *Stoked!* (Allen & Unwin, 1994), *Radical Take-offs* (Allen & Unwin, 1994) and *Mosh* (Random House, 1996). His next book, *Sad Boys*, is a novel of lost innocence set on Rottnest Island.

Leonie Stevens was born during the Cuban Missile Crisis. At the age of eleven, frustrated by the plot limitations of 'Lost in Space', she wrote her first story. After some years of variously working, writing and watching daytime soaps, Leonie's first novel, *Nature Strip*, was published in 1994. Since then her stories have been appearing in magazines, anthologies, on radio and the net, and her second novel, *Big Man's Barbie*, was published in 1996. She loves Black Grape and Scorcese films, and currently lives in Melbourne, where she is working on her third novel, *Glue*, as well as watching daytime soaps.

Kathleen Stewart was born in Sydney in 1958. She is the author of several works of fiction: *Waiting Room*, *Victim Train*, *Louis: A Normal Novel* and *Spilt Milk*, which was short-listed for the 1995 New South Wales Premier's Literary Awards. Her first collection of poetry, *Snow*, was short-listed for the 1994 Banjo Awards, and the 1994 *Age* Book of the Year. Her most recent novel is *Nightflowers*.

Kirsten Tranter's writing and artwork have appeared in several publications including *RePublica*, *Hermes*,

PUB FICTION

Tangent (an anthology of women writers from Sydney University), the Varuna New Poetry broadsheet series, *Picador New Writing 3* and *Ready or Not*. In 1993 she edited *Tangent* and has worked on a number of student publications. Kirsten lives in Sydney's inner west. She hopes that one day shandies will become fashionable again.

Christos Tsiolkas, born in 1965, is five foot eleven inches, naturally a brunette and drives a 1977 Chrysler Sigma. He lives in Collingwood and spends his time writing, staffing the desk at the Cinemedia Library and attending as many films as he possibly can. His first novel, *Loaded*, was published by Random House in 1995 and his second book, *Jump Cuts*, a collaboration with Sasha Soldatow, was published by Random in 1996. Christos has had short stories, film reviews, polemical raves and essays published in a variety of magazines, anthologies, fanzines and student newspapers.

Anne Maree Weatherall was born in Brisbane the year television came to Australia and wrote her first book titled *Piano Pony* at age ten. She has published various short stories and poems with student magazines and anthologies such as U and Us 3. She is currently finishing a novel called *Whacking It Up*.